The Rowdyman

The Rowdyman

a novel by
Gordon Pinsent

McGraw-Hill Ryerson Limited

Toronto   Montreal   New York   London
Sydney   Johannesburg   Mexico   Panama
Düsseldorf   Singapore   São Paulo
Kuala Lumpur   New Delhi

THE ROWDYMAN

© Gordon Pinsent, 1973

ISBN 0-07-077663-6

Library of Congress Catalog Card Number
73-14395

1 2 3 4 5 6 7 8 9 0 D-73 2 1 0 9 8 7 6 5 4 3

Printed and bound in Canada

To Charmion
Who creates by being

ANDREW SCOTT

The last human voice I ever heard was Will's, and his foolish laughing face was the last to leave its imprint on my absolutely final conscious moment in this world as Andrew Scott.

And even after what happened, I'm still his friend. Perhaps his only friend. If that sounds wrong, I'll just say that I've been around him more than anyone else. I'm his only other pair of socks. He's not wearing them at the moment, but they're there if he needs them.

His friend. Not many can say that. Ruth maybe, and Williams. Ruth, because she can't stand to see him hurt. That's a friendly thing. Williams has put him in jail on occasion. That's not friendly, unless you know Williams. He's a friend. He was a friend. Williams is dead. He was an old constable who should have been something else. A shepherd or something. Will's family, three sisters and two brothers, being in charge of his aches and pains, haven't much time to be friendly, but on the other hand, they haven't had him committed.

I already said that I was Will's friend. I guess I'm proud of it. I couldn't say that to him, naturally, but if he reads this and sees I haven't mentioned it, he'll wonder. He's doubtful of many things these days, and he never used to be. Things have happened. His head is in turmoil, and it shouldn't be. That head, fine and foolish, that harboured only happy thoughts, is confused. In danger of being lost to us. And his heart has shrunk. I know, because I've seen it much bigger.

I've never cried in my life, you know that? I've never found anything to cry about. Until now. Will Cole of 9 Fourth Avenue, Grand Falls, Newfoundland, Canada, five feet ten, of the Anglican faith at a wedding or funeral, can make you do that. Cry—he can also drive you right off the head. I don't suppose I would have been born if he could take care of himself. Hell, there are things I can say about

1

myself. I should be telling *my* story. Or somebody else should. But I'm telling his. Know why that is? You want to know? I'm one of these people who looks as though he hasn't got a story. Well, that's all right with me because I save all the important things to say to myself—and sometimes to him.

So Will, my son, how do you like all this attention you're getting. "That's a nice jacket Will." "How ya getting on Will." "Some good to see you." You're a bugger Will. There's no limit to your demands on life and on a buddy's patience. You can't expect people to be nice all the time for God's sake. There are other things beside laughter. Who do you think you are? GROW UP! And be what? (According to his sister Mary, he should make a stab at being normal for a start.) "Put on a tie and go to church for God's sake. All right, don't go to church. Just walk up the street with Ruth Lowe on your arm so someone might say: 'Here comes Will Cole, and he's clean.'"

Don't listen to it Will. They don't understand. I'm not altogether sure that I do either, but if there's something you want to do, do it. Your way. Mind you, it even surprises me, that you find that many things to be happy about. Why do you think you got into such trouble at school? No teacher wants their students to be *that* happy, for God's sake. I never saw anything funny about school. You found it funny when you failed. And Miss Bishop blamed me for cutting her foot-long strap in half, and while she was giving it to me with the remaining six inches there you were choking with laughter at the back of the room.

Some friend you are, my son. Never mind, better it's me than some guy who'd punch you out because he didn't understand you. Keep on the lookout for that, Will. You'll keep running into people who won't understand you. Someone may even tell you they don't like you, someday, believe it or not. When it happens, laugh. The way you do with everything else. Some people are like that, b'y. And like anywhere, some good, some bad. Just like anywhere. But the bad won't see the good in you.

Know where it's tough on you, Will? And you can't blame

2

anyone for this. The people in Grand Falls have to get on with it. And it's the same anywhere. How many do you know who are still content with taking molasses in their tea instead of sugar? And you remember drinking—what the hell was the name of that stuff—Postum! Remember that? Anyway, a range is better than the old woodstove, hey? A fridge is a goddamn sight better than having to climb down the cellar steps for your spuds and turnips. I broke my neck once a week at least. You're getting impatient with me, so—anyway—they just don't have time to stop and laugh with you as much anymore. I mean, you'll laugh at anything.

There are things to do. We got to get going, Will. I know what you'd like now. A bottle of Haig Ale at the candy store. So would I. Or a hamburger at MacPherson's. I know. We've had better since, but they'll never taste that way again.

Anyway. You don't change, Will, my son. Don't ask me if that's a sin. I can't keep up with it myself, but that's me. And we're talking about you.

I never told you what Wilf Anstey's young fellow said to me when I went to St. John's to see my mother's sister last May. Carol and me were driving from the airport with him —a snot like that, driving for God's sake. Remember when driving a car used to be a big deal? Anyway. He asked me if I smoked. And I said, "No, I gave it up three years ago." Know what? He was talking about marijuana. Grass. I can't get used to it as fast as that. And I want to. The changes. I won't be able to handle them. I know I won't, but—well there you are. I said, "No, I've never smoked grass, but Will Cole and me slept in it often enough." Hey buddy, you wait till Wilf Anstey's son discovers dried chokecherry leaves rolled in the Grand Falls *Advertiser*.

* * * * *

"LOVELY, TELL YOUR MOTHER." The young girl was reminded of her prettiness, it was easy to tell that, by the special little way she looked at Will. Her smile was prepared, if you know what I mean. One that she only used on boys

3

her own age, not on a character like Will, in greasy work-clothes and tangled hair. "Oh, shut up, Will." She flicked her shiny hair back onto her shoulder, improved her chest-line by correcting her posture and kept right on going. Confident that Will's eyes would follow her down the street, through her gate into her house, and up to her bedroom, where no man or boy had ever been.

That particular girl who went by the name of Ellen Rowsell, lived right next door to Will and his family—mother, Mary, Hilda and Leah, his sisters, and Tom and Lon, his brothers, all older. To tell the truth, her bedroom was right across the lane from Will's. Hers was a very dark little bedroom because the blind was always down. It needn't have been because Will Cole is not a peeping Tom. He's some things but he's not a peeping Tom. He's everything, but not a peeping Tom. He'd come down a chimney or up through a drain pipe to take advantage of anything female—but you won't catch him looking through windows. No, my son, that's what you won't.

I don't have any brothers or sisters, so you can find me at Will's place, if you want me. I'll be wearing a new V-neck sweater from the Royal Stores and Will is the one with the snotty nose and the worn breeches. Besides that, though, you can tell us apart because he's Batman and I'm Robin. He's ten and I'm ten and Ruth is eight. She's Uptown. Will and me are Downtown.

"Get up off yer arse, my son, an' go get a bucket of water for yer *mudder*." Will's father died when Will and me were about twelve, and when we looked down at him, small and frail in his coffin, which had been placed across the dining room table for all to see, his sandy hair and unfurrowed brow made a liar of his living image. And those small hook boots could never have done the damage that he claimed they could if ever they connected with us. Completely unlike the black-eyed giant with the stiff collar and derby hat, who shouted us on our way with water bucket, dragging.

And cold? Don't be talkin'. With our two bare hands wrapped around that steel handle and that icy water pouring out of the lion's mouth, half in the bucket and half on

4

our hands. And miserable going back to the house? Stumbling and staggering with that jesus-big bucket, now only half-full, skinning out our knee joints each time we tried to get in a fair-sized forward step with our right and left legs. And icy roads? Cursing and swearing, with running noses, which up to that time supplied the only breakfast we'd been offered. Up on the back bridge and into the house.

"COAL," says his Mother. "Holy sufferin'," says Will and out we go into the woodshed. Back into the kitchen. "WOOD," says his sister Mary. "Holy jumpin'," says Will, flinging open the storm door. "He can manage, Andrew b'y. Sit down over there by the window an' have some porridge, now." I didn't tell Mrs. Cole I'd already had some at my house, so I tucked in with the others to the tune of young Will's reluctant axe out in the back yard. Then, in he came. More messed up than ever. Brown hair everywhere, both nostrils running free, creating twin scarlet trails from his nose to his mouth, one sock lower than the other, and his half-wool, half-holes sweater hooked on a splinter from the "splits" in his arms. He dropped the wood and almost rammed his red hands into the damper hole on the top of the woodstove to get them back to life.

Will grinned. "How's dat?" "Look at how wet it is," said Mary. "What's the matter with you, atall?" Will had a great talent for ignoring anything uncomplimentary about himself. "Dat's da WATER an' da WOOD an' da COAL. Where's me dime?" His mother announced that she had, as a matter of fact, promised him a dime. His Father said: "I knew there was someting ta make him move that fast. Sit down to your breakfast, now."

"I don't want no breakfast, I wants me dime."

"After breakfast."

"I'll sit here an' wait."

"NOW, LOOK."

"All right, Pop."

He sat very quickly. Mary smoothed his hair. I asked him what he was going to do with his dime. "Goin' to the Nickel, Saturday." Mary warned him that it was a Loretta Young picture with kissing from the beginning to the end, and why doesn't he buy himself a comic book. "Read 'em all but Plastic Man, an' I don't like him." Somewhere around here, his brother Lon dragged his sleeve through his porridge while reaching for a slice of raisin bread. And all paid little or no attention as he examined his elbow, with disgust. Except Will, who had pushed himself slightly away from the table on his chair's back legs, his face frozen in silent laughter, until out of his man-sized mouth came a squeak —then another, which trailed off into a peal that all but shattered his porridge bowl; but no more so than the fart that followed. This sent him to the Morrocan couch in the corner where he flopped to kick out the rest of his laugh, with his arms around his middle. After each different sounding laugh, you could count on a different sounding fart, until at the last, we thought we'd have to get him to the hospital. But instead, we finished our breakfast.

I didn't have a dime, so it was Will's turn to bum one from one of the grownups once he got inside. The only grownups foolish enough to tangle with that theatre full of ragged-arsed little animals were millworkers on the four o'clock shift. So the matinees were the only chance to see the weekly picture. Will didn't find a dime for me and got caught up in Tarzan. I spent the whole time freezing my small bum on the cold stone steps, still damp from the morning rainfall. I made one attempt to get past the ticket man in the lobby. Marky Cahil was old, and had poor eyes, but not poor enough to suit me.

All I needed was one big person to "take me in" as a relative, and I would be sitting in there next to Will, sharing the old gum that he'd collected from under the seats. Some of it would have been there since last Labour Day, and had about as much flavour to it as ten-year-old putty, but leave it to Will to separate the spearmint or doublemint from the juicy fruit (he didn't like juicy fruit). But there was I on the outside, without a relative.

Will was never stuck for a relative if he didn't have a dime. Very unlikely looking relatives all of them, and not one of them legitimate. His own sisters and brothers have never talked to him in public, let alone taken him into the pictures. So Will found his own. He had the record for the most brothers and sisters. A different one each Saturday for a year. That makes fifty-two, but of course they all looked like the same person to Marky's old eye.

The town hall-cum-theatre, despite its majestical dominance over High Street, had only a handful of "plush" seats to its name. Those were a bit more expensive, and the only child found there was "Billy Brown, from Uptown," with little white shirt, little bow tie and little blue suit, and a bloody big mother, who kept combing his hair, which was blond. No, by God, it was almost white. You know the kind? He almost looked like a little old man. In fact his old man brought him once, and he wasn't that much bigger than Billy, which from a distance made them look either like two of them albinos or "twin brudders from da moon," as Will put it. Whatever, with their chalk white faces and white hair, back there in their plush seats, they made a pretty good beacon to head for in the dark when you wanted to go back for a pee.

The other one who used to sit back there was Ruth, until, as time went along and her crush on Will became more and more noticeable, she made her way, row by row, down almost to the hard seats where she was to have her toes squashed by the seat ahead like the rest of us.

"LOOK OUT BEHIND YA!" "GIVE IT TO 'EM!" "PUNCH HIM IN DA CHOPS!" Without Will's front row direction, Don Winslow of the Navy; Herman Brix, the Hawk of the Wilderness; and Nyoka, Queen of the Jungle wouldn't have made it to the next Saturday. But when Deanna Durbin threw herself on her bed and cried herself foolish for her old boy friend with the big waves in his head, who would take off up the aisle with a "TAHDIDDERAH" and slap his hips in his near perfect impression of The Painted Stallion? Then, with almost unbelieveable eyesight, outguess and dodge the outstretched legs that one by one shot out in his path to prevent his return? And he'd make it, laughing like his gut would burst, until his laugh, high and clear when his day began but now like a twenty-cent bazooka, came to

7

a choking halt; to be replaced by an expression that tells us he's either messed his pants or he's caught sight of the little girl from uptown—looking at him, from a few seats away. "Holy jumpin'!"

Seconds before the lights went up we'd make for the big front doors that clanged open, loosing the nest of kids, who scrambled in every direction, squinting from the too-real afternoon sunlight.

For Will and me and a couple of others, it meant down to the woods and the Tarzan tree. A spruce, tall (the base was twenty feet below us) limbed out and equipped with a very long thin rope. Only the strong of arm and the small of brain could pull off what happened next. You'd stand on the bank, with rope in hand, run off the bank and attempt an accurate swing round the tree. If it didn't work, you'd stand a pretty good chance of running straight into the wall of jagged bedrock on the opposite side of the dip. You'd hope, though, to let go of the rope before that and fall to the cushion of boulders and sticks below. We had one fellow who was pretty good at that.

"Hey Roger, come on my son," Will hands the rope to the frailest kid of all. "You gets first swing. Do it at an angle now. Don't forget. Why don't ya go?" "I hurt meself last time." "You won't have dat same trouble dis time. Way ya go, now. Dat's it. Get ready—GO!" Roger does what he's told. "I CAN TELL YA RIGHT NOW, ROG, DAT YA DIDN'T DO IT RIGHT." Roger forgoes the pleasure of piling into the wall of rock; and for that matter the boulders at the tree base twenty feet below don't catch his fancy either; so he chooses to hang onto the rope and wind himself completely around the tree until he's out of rope. He hugs the tree for dear life. "COME DOWN DA TREE, MY SON" says Will. "I CAN'T. THE INSIDES OF ME LEGS IS ALL RAW." But he skins down, anyway. A squeal with every skin, reopening all sorts of old wounds from earlier Saturdays. Then scales the red-earth bank and, wetfaced, squeals his way towards home, slope-shouldered and bowlegged, looking a bit like a reamed-out leprechaun.

"Oh God, look at who's here," someone says. Ruth Lowe and a downtown girl friend stop to help Roger to his feet after he falls to his knees in a cow platter.

Will, never one to turn away an audience, especially "Root" Lowe, jams his hands in his pockets and swaggers over to the rope. Makes a grab for it, misses, gets it on the second swoop and walks back for a good start, with many a subtle glance to the women. Well, Jesus, when the time is right, he takes off for the edge, with a style that would make old Johnny Weissmuller chuck away his trophies, flings himself off the slope, screams something fierce, soars through the air, circles the pole and lands back on the bank. His plan to land on one foot didn't work out too well, but his twisted ankle didn't hurt unless he stood on it, and there he was, grinning like a fool, straight at the girls. Waiting for his applause. He drops the rope, jams his hands back in his pockets, flashes Ruth his "nothing to it" shrug, Ruth smiles and the other one says, "Come on, let's go," and they move away.

Will, although still grinning, has a tear on his cheek, and it's only when the girls are well on their way that he painfully extracts his hands from his pockets. They are still curled up in rope-holding fashion. He doubles up a little bit and tries to uncurl them.

He didn't show the damage to the others but from what I could see I knew goddamn well he should have wrapped the rope around his hands before his famous flight. "Dey're all rined out! Dey're all rined out!" was what I thought he kept saying all along the pipeline to Fourth Avenue.

Because of his rined-out hands, Miss Bishop, our teacher, excused him from the Arithmetic test. "Thanks," she said. "Tanks" said Will. "It's not TANKS, Will, and it's not DESE, DEM or DOSE. It's THESE, THEM, THOSE, and it's THANKS, and so on. Actually thank you is even better. Stop jumping around when I'm talking to you. See what I mean by good manners? That's better. You're not excused. Now where do you want to go?" "To da tilet fer a pee, tank you." "GO," she said. "No, dat was just den," said Will. I

9

could tell that our teacher was just about to call him something filthy by the way she raised her shoulders and tightened her fists, but then I realized that that's what you do when you're standing in water, so she removed her feet with the practical shoes from that unhallowed spot and returned to her desk, saying "Go get the janitor," through her teeth.

When she read out our Easter marks one month later, she still hadn't quite forgotten the incident. You could tell by the tone of her voice whenever she had something to say to Will.

"I see no reason to keep you on the edge of your seats." I looked back at Will and he was frozen with fear. "First of all, I want to say that you children have done yourselves proud this year. Most of you, anyway." Will, expecting the worst, was all set to lift the lid of his desk and puke on his Captain Marvel comic books.

"That leaves a few of you who have been rather a disappointment to me, and I'm sure to your parents. Had those few studied harder, they could now share the excitement of top honours with their classmates. However, they chose to devote their precious time to play and not to work." She's looking straight at my friend. "To drawing rude pictures of the Lone Ranger and Tonto and selling them for ten cents apiece. Not very well drawn either, I might add; passing notes—laughing—cutting my strap in two pieces." Here she looked at me, still misinformed. Then back to Will: "—making rude noises—emptying inkwells and filling them with—YOU TAKE THAT FOOLISH GRIN OFF YOUR FACE." Now, here, she could still have been looking at Will, but it was hard to tell because when she got this mad she lost control of her eyes and appeared to be accusing everyone, which momentarily took the weight off the "saucy little nipper" who was causing great harm to his insides by holding back what was his most natural human talent. Laughter. And lots of it. But he had to be careful. When her eyes went funny, he knew that next she would bite down hard on her tongue (once, till it bled), turn her toes inward, pick

10

up the nearest pointer, and come stomping down the aisle, looking for a spindly back to bust it on.

However, she said she was happy to tell us that there were no failures. Well, you talk about a racket! Will let out a victory shout that sounded like Ahhhh-hhhhhhaaa-a-a-aha-ha-ha-hahahahaha, and started congratulating himself by shaking everyone's hands.

"I'm glad to see you're happy Will. You were one of the children I was talking about." Will was nothing short of amazed: "Don't tell me I got top marks! Wha-a-a?" Instead of telling him that, she told him that he got fifty. In fact, she said that she'd been up all night, had searched everywhere to get him forty-nine, but she had to make it fifty. "BUT, IT'S THE SMALLEST FIFTY IN THE CLASS." Will didn't care. Fifty is fifty. His favourite number. He was still grinning and feeling on a par with Principal Cramm when Ruth smiled at him, and, at the sound of the bell, watched him pile up his books and saunter to the door and out, with all the time in the world. This was the first and last time he was ever seen to linger on the grounds; he even stopped to discuss it all with his "equals." Uptowners, included. But as nice as it was, he was pretty sure of a rough time when he came back, and in fact, there had been nothing but rough times since Miss Bishop.

(This hasn't anything to do with anything, but Will loved Miss Bishop.) Anyway, it doesn't matter. It couldn't be much longer. How many more fifties were in him? And, "HOLY JUMPIN', DAT ROTTEN TING IS PASSIN' ME NOTES NOW." Ruth Lowe didn't mind being "dat rotten ting." It was bad enough for Will that they were starting to put the two of them together at school, but now that the news had spread to Fourth Avenue and to his very house, it was just about time to run away.

He punched the woodshed, being much kinder to it the second time. He was supposed to be hitting his next oldest brother, Lon, who, according to him had been covering the whole downtown with Will-Ruth love tales.

"I can't go nowhere now," he squealed. "Dey even writes it on da sides of buildings—an' fences—an' ever'ting. An'

I don't like 'er. I HATES 'ER. WHY DON'T DEY WRITE DAT NOW AN' AGAIN?" I could see that we'd never get to play our "Goods and Bads" until he got his brother out of his system. He thought he might put something in Lon's bed, but since it was his own bed too, he went on to something else.

Lon swung open the screen door and gave Will's dirty look right back to him. "What's the matter with you?" Then, as Will and I slipped away behind the woodshed at Will's head gesture (which always had a lot of Boston Blackie in it), Lon just stood there on the back bridge, taking in the neighbour's fence. Not that Blackman's fence was that handsome, but it was Lon's middle-distance, out-of-focus point for that moment and maybe longer. Lon liked middle distance. One Christmas, I almost saw him black out from staring at a tree light for close to two hours. But the light went out before he did. I saw it.

"I tink I'll be Tom Mix if he stays dere long enough," Will was whispering. "Watch dis." I watched, as he got to the woodshed roof by the telephone pole cable, heard him scamper across the hot and bubbling tarpaper, (which must have added to his already rotten humour); then as I backed off, I saw him stand and prepare to jump off onto his brother's back. Tom Mix would have been proud, until, as he left the edge, scared as hell but committed, his brother had the bad manners to come out of his trance and walk away. "COME BACK," said Will, mid-air, but Lon didn't come back at all. In fact, he went up the road to a girl's house, the only thing important enough to make him give up half a trance. Will has that back bridge to the woodshed to thank for his flat feet and his boomerang legs. He landed, buckled at the knees and got off a few choice remarks from his froglike position before Lon got completely out of sight. "I MISSED ON PURPOSE!" and, "DON'T YOU GO WRITIN' YOU-KNOW-WHAT ON ANY MORE FENCES!" and, "CAN'T COUNT ON YOU FOR ANYTING!"

* * * * *

I would have been content to sit and listen to Will's eldest sister Hilda play the old-fashioned organ; "Long Long Ago" made Will's mother feel more like darning the pyramid of socks that she had in her lap, but Will wanted to move. "Mom, can I have a slice of lassey bread?" "Yes, b'y. Soon's I finish this one." "Can I have it now? 'Cause we're goin' over to Harvey's an' Henry's." Hilda told him to get it himself, which was just enough to make Will say that he no longer wanted it. "Hardly stubborn," said Hilda and carried on singing and playing.

"What are we havin' for tea?"

"Baked beans."

"Holy dyin', not again. I don't want any. I'll eat over at Harvey's and Henry's."

It was then that Hilda suggested he go up to Ruth Lowe's for supper, and wasn't that her name? Ruth? Will turned white.

"What're ya talkin' about, maid, I don't know anyone called dat." His voice was too squeaky to be convincing.

I think it was Mary who came in next. "My, it's some nice out today." Or was it Leah, the youngest sister? No, it was Mary. Leah was already there somewhere. Mary put her prayer book and Easter hat and gloves on the table. "Guess who I saw at church—Mr. and Mrs. Lowe." She had a little look at my friend—"and Ruth." Will flips the pages of his Batman comic book so vigorously he rips one page right out. "You know her don't you Will?" Will's voice is so loud it cracks in a hundred places. "WHAT? WHO? I DON'T KNOW NO ROOT."

It would be almost too cruel to say that his oldest brother Tom knew about it as well, but the grin on Lon's face, as the two of them came into the front room, might suggest it to be true. "Guess who came down the road just ahead of us. Ruth Lowe." "YOU BEEN TELLIN' EVER'BODY, 'AVEN'T YA?" Lon shielded his face as Will climbed over family to get to him.

After as long as it took to get them apart—"She's ugly. I hates dat ting. She's a rotten rat, an' if anyone talks about it again, I'm takin' off." Mary manages to get him by a woolen sleeve. "Oh, now, we were only playing, sure."

After he'd pulled away from Mary and we'd run outside,

13

he got inside the cold cellar through the outside hatch and told me to replace the hatch door, fix the hasps in place, and go home. I did all of that because he was my friend, and I didn't want a small rock in the head the next morning first thing.

He stayed in there for the longest time. It's black in there. I know. He's brave, Will is. "Dark. Don't see any rats." His father had told him there were hundreds of them in there. Will figured he just didn't want all the turnips and cabbage chewed up by the kids. "I hates rats. Lots of spuds and turnips but no rats. Dey're probably not too big anyway." He thought for a second he saw one but it turned out to be his boot and the tail was a dragging lace.

In the kitchen Lon drapes his left arm over the gothic-shaped top of the Stewart Warner radio and punches it in the face with his right. That, and "Bloody old thing," usually guaranteed him a couple of almost crystal clear seconds of a Maple Leaf game, or, as was now the case, "Inner Sanctum." Mary wonders if Will would be at Harvey's and Henry's but Tom arrives. "Not at Harvey's and Henry's." Will's mom goes to put the kettle on. Lon, tired of eating his nails: "Mom, can I have a piece of raisin bread?" The gentle lady looks at the kettle first, almost apologetically, and goes inside the pantry for the raisin bread.

"I think he's down in the cold cellar. I heard a small noise." Mary is gentle. "Will? You in there b'y?" Tom sounds a bit like his Father. "We hear you. Come on out!" Will's voice is small. "No, ya'll hit me." Hilda and Leah speak at once and assure him that he'll be all right. Mr. Cole shoots them an "I'll-decide that" look from his chair at the table, while Tom gets down and peers into and around the dark. "No sir, brudder, ya won't catch me up dere. Not till ya tells Lon ta stop chewin' his gums about her an' me. She's a rotten little rat, dat's all she is." "COME OUT". "What time is it?" They all say "Eleven." By now, he's tickled to death with the attention. "Who's out dere? Mom and Hild? You dere? They answer. "Leah?" "Yes, an' gettin' fed up with this." "Mary an' Tom?" Mary says yes and Tom swears, and Will would know Tom's voice anyway, so he

14

lets it suffice. "AND EVEN LON". "YA-S-S-S." Then the negotiations: He wants supper, with two pieces of raspberry pie, two dimes, Lon's side of the bed, a trip to the Fox Farm on a day of his choice, a small dog, preferably a crackie, and fourteen comic books. His last request seemed to lack a bit of superiority, because he heard Leah say, "Here comes Pop. Now he'll get it."

"YOU GET OUT OF THE CELLAR OR I'LL GIVE YA THE BOOT." Nothing could be plainer than that, but still the nipper made him wait. "No. I'm goin' ta stay down here till dat rotten ting dies." "UP HERE." "NO." "Suit yourself." He closes the trap. "POP. Dere are no rats down here, are dere?" "No, my son, just snakes." That night—

Will only had one piece of pie, no dimes, no crackie, no trip to the Fox Farm, no comic books, and he didn't get Lon's side of the bed, which was the outside and would have allowed him easy escape from his brother's long toe-nails. Lon left these long on purpose. They came in handy when Will would decide to grab more than his share of blankets and sheets during any one of those typically bum-freezing Newfie winter nights, when tempers and summer love and the woodstove cooled down. But not before the once frozen fingers of Will's mitts had uncurled and dripped themselves dry for tomorrow, when he would take on the world in a snowball fight.

* * * * *

I commented on the young things, one in particular, as we looked in at the Friday night Legion dance for young people. "Get your eyes off dat," Will warned. "Sure, dat's only fifteen. Dat's a walkin' twenty lashes, dat is."

I wanted to go home. The two hours sleep I got the night before and the night's beer intake had just about done me in, but Will was as sparkly-eyed as a frigging owl, and we had to check out the billiard room in his search for a little lustre on this dull night. Will wanted a game but the long list of waiting names on the chalkboard discouraged him, so he settled for a beer. He took it with him to a corner chair, sipped it and waited for the club manager to discover

15

him and turf him out as a nonmember. The previous Saturday Will had his membership taken away from him when his billiard cue accidently slipped out of his hands and broke Norm Hiscock's glasses, while he was wearing them.

But what a big friendly grin he was giving the manager now. Forgiving him for everything. As the manager made a move for Will, Will pointed to me. I showed my card and signed Will in as a guest. Which, in Will's case, was only barely allowable. The manager had another shot of screech and tried to forget it by turning his back on the room and concentrating on the dance in the opposite section. He shouldn't have. But I was there, and I always tell the truth. Will didn't start it. He remarked about Kevin Hall's shooting after Kevin had ordered the TV turned down—that it might throw off his shot: "Anyting for an excuse, eh, Kevin?" said Will. Kevin answered with "Shut your gob, Will," and slid back his cue to shoot, with the kind of style and concentration that won him his private cue and private sheath. "Kiss me arse, Kevin," said Will. "Shit!" said Kevin. But surprisingly enough, it didn't start until Fred Squires commented on Will's sister Mary's "very nice" chest.

There isn't a thing about Will that's private (and that's for sure), except his family.

When Williams arrived, late but eager and the manager had shouted his almost hysterical complaints into his ear, he reassembled his bulk and followed the trail of pointing fingers to the toilet, whereupon he raised his boot to strike. Williams's boot looks a bit like Williams's face—big, square and covered with a whole army of tiny scars brought on by broken beer bottles on VE day. His nose, with nary a pore, was either put on by a bad plastic surgeon or a schoolboy with plasticene. This whole thing was topped off by the sweetest pair of Nelson Eddy eyebrows.

When the manager said, "TAKE OFF THE HINGES, DON'T BREAK MY DOOR," Williams's boot was already poised, and to lower it then would have made him look foolish.

Will saw him come through and barely had time to submerge Fred's head in the toilet and bang down the flush handle before Williams was upon him. "Get outa there," he said to poor old Fred, yanking him aside, and not stopping at the sound of Fred's head on the tile. He might have followed Will over the cubicle wall into the next toilet but his big boot slipped into the bowl and splashed him to the knee.

Will was already out of there and under the card table in the next room. "Tell him I'm not here, Denny." "He's here," said Denny, as Williams rounded the corner. Will raised up with a scream, and sprinkled the small room with the winnings and losings and ashes and beer. Williams's body had slowed down a lot but his long arm was as fast as ever, and it came back with a small piece of Will's shirt, as Will bounced up and down the walls of that crowded room like a jack rabbit—looking for the opening; he found it and the two of them took off down the hall, through the cloakroom and onto the dance floor, where Will (barely escaping Williams's most ambitious lunge) crouched, weaved, and shielded himself behind the dancers, not even stopping for a quick feel, on his route to the door.

Will's laughter had a touch of panic in it now, and he must have been going thirty when he flattened Mr. and Mrs. Boone and their daughter Sheila who should have come in the out door while Will was going out the in. Williams kept the family well tramped down and I didn't help much either, but they were soon to straighten themselves out. Mr. Boone had hoped to play a game of cards, but instead he had to dance every dance with his daughter, keeping her torn dress together at the back. But it was all right. She wouldn't have been asked by anyone else anyway, with a face like that.

As for the rest, they put the card room back in shape, which was more than they could do for Fred, who stood still dripping against the door frame. Someone ventured that he didn't smell as good as he might. "It could have been worse," said Fred.

I waited while Will and Williams circled the Legion hall again. "Dick, get your hand out of there," said Williams as he passed a couple of hot young bodies in the shadows, and kept right on. Will's distant shouts made him get up a touch

17

more of the reserve steam: "Better lay off da beer, old man" and "Knees up, knees up, knees up."

I'll be goddamned if the old man didn't catch him. He could have taken a shorter route to the station, but seeing the United Church doors open and the Friday night crowd coming out, he thought he'd parade Will along in front for all to see and appreciate. He thought he'd throw in a couple of extra grunts to colour his performance but found he didn't have to. In fact he was almost sorry he wheezed and grunted as much as he did. It might have made him look old. The thought of it made him give a little extra heist on Will's arm, locked safely behind his shoulder blade. "Christ, Williams," said Will. Ron Cobb thought he'd help, "GOOD FOR YOU WILLIAMS. THROW AWAY THE KEY." Will tried to get at him but Williams held him fast. "Hello, Root," had a lot of pain in it. He was being whistled by so fast he didn't see her smile at him. Neither did her mother.

"He spoke to you," Mrs. Lowe said, still using her church voice. It would have been better if Hitler had passed by. As far as I was concerned, Ruth was now a bit too old to be living at home. Pretty though. Some pretty. Not too smart though. She was still waiting for Will. Why this girl, with a car of her own and a dress for every day in the week, still wanted that ragged-arsed individual I wouldn't take time to figure out. I know one thing. There were times when I would've delivered him down her bloody chimney just to get him away from me. Jesus, he made me mad. Yes you did, Will. I had problems too, you know. I was getting married, I was still on shift work at the mill and the arse was out of my pants.

I said Hello to Ruth. "Now, who was that?" "Andrew Scott, a friend of Will's." "I don't understand it. He spoke to you too." "They went to school together. Don't worry about it." Mr. Lowe was helping, but Mrs. Lowe didn't want to hear about it.

What happened inside the station was too fast for my slow head, but between the jigs and the reels, we were out of there and retracing our steps at a much greater rate of speed than when we'd arrived, and Williams, now boiled

18

over and collapsed on his night duty cot, would have to wait a bit longer for the "tricky little bugger" to run out of steam. And that certainly wouldn't be tonight. There was a lot of ground to cover before our eight o'clock shift and already Williams had taken up too much of the night.

Will drove, and I haven't heard such sounds come out of my brother Cec's truck. I told him to keep it at twenty. "He's nervous. Ha-ha-a-a! Don't wet yerself Andrew. I'll get ya dere. Straight as an arrow."

He had mentioned some party somewhere, but he wasn't absolutely sure which house it was. Don't ask me why he decided to leave the road and rip out a dozen or so pickets from Alf Morrow's fence, but as I caught sight of Alf's size seventeen neck at his bedroom window, I felt the need to cover up my features. Will fought with the gears. He laughed so hard through all of this, he was almost too weak to get us off the fence. It took the sight of Alf's silhouette in his open front door to do the trick, and this time he did see us. "TALK TO YOU ABOUT THAT IN THE MORNING ALF," I shouted as we backed up onto the road and got the hell away from there.

The party had run down and so had the man of the house. And his daughter Marie was worn out to the knees by Will's dancing. Justin, the girl's fiancé, chewed nuts and waited for a word from his future father-in-law.

I was the record-changer. "ANDREW, GIVE US A TREMBLER!" but before I was able to find a slow enough number, her father had something to say. "Time to go to bed." "Good enough," says Will and pretends to follow his daughter. She gets to her room, and closes the door. Justin brushes his hands free of nut dust and moves forward. "I'd like to know who invited you two anyway." "This one could smell a party in Botwood," I said, as I checked out the fiancé. "Let's go, my son. It's over. We got to be to work at eight."

The man should have left it at that, but he thought a little punch on Will's arm would do him some good. Will laughed. "What're ya goin' to do, skipper, throw me out?" The shove that followed, sent Will backwards on his ass. I

19

could feel myself get sick. That happens when Will gets hurt. I stepped in front of the man and, out of the corner of my eye, saw Justin go for Will. "I'll get him out, Mr. Perry."

"Let go of him, Justin."

It was my slamming him against the wall that brought the guitar from it's hanging place, that gave Will the idea to use it on Justin, that gave Justin the idea to duck, that wrote off the guitar on the corner of the TV. "You'll pay for that brother, that was thirty-five dollars that was." Will answered the older man by swinging at him (laughing, by the way). I got my friend around the waist and Justin punched my friend in the nose, squirting my friend's blood all over my face; and Will still treated the whole thing as a game. Everyone else was serious. Especially Justin who just got one of Will's boots in his "morning glories."

We dragged and tumbled and ripped and swore our way to the door. The man of the house very kindly opened it for us and as a last minute gesture of hospitality, kicked us out into the early morning. Justin would have continued but he had lost his audience. Besides, Will only gave him to the count of three to get going, before he pelted him with small stones. Justin ran slower than Will counted.

We washed ourselves off in a small cold pond on our way back to Grand Falls. Up to our belts in the grey mist. And quiet? Like a boneyard. Which Will can't stand, so he starts to giggle, and before you knew it the both of us are carrying on something foolish. Splashing, going under, and making a mockery of the peaceful, silent night.

I dragged myself on shore, quite satisfied that I'd had enough foolishness for one night, and I got in my brother's truck and waited for Will to laugh himself out. The sight of him out there. Still fighting the sunrise, oblivious to my remark that it was quarter to shift time, and happy. Genuinely, childishly, happy.

RUTH LOWE

I should have stayed in the bank a while longer, because I'd only had one glass of champagne, and it wasn't every day that one of us fifteen people had a baby; and Allan Sparks was a nice man to work for; but there was Will, climbing out of the truck. Same place as usual, but maybe a few seconds earlier today.

I gulped down the last drop of champagne and strolled out to see him. "Hi," I shouted. Wouldn't you know, I was the one who had to cross the street? "How are da Girl Guides?" For some reason, that particular reference always got to me. Maybe because I associated it with immaturity— or worse, a kind of hopeless purity. The black stockings, the fortress-like blue bloomers, and the starched-up tunics, impossible to wrinkle, although, I knew a couple of girls who managed.

I kind of apologized for not speaking to him in front of the church on his way to jail. Mom wouldn't have understood. He waited for me to explain my mother to him all over again, but I didn't care to. "Call me some evening when you're not drinking."

He allowed as there weren't too many of those evenings left, but he'd certainly remember my asking. He said he hadn't run out of downtowners yet. That he'd probably get to the uptowners by January first and I'd be first or second on the list. "But I won't be takin' ya to da pictures, y'know. Or singin' songs 'round your mudder's piano, or drinkin' cokes. No, my love, not if da Girl Guides want to play wit' da grownups in da tall grass. Let's see how yer doin'. Give us a kiss. Come on. Right on da old mout'."

He thought I'd retreat, but, if anything, I advanced, poised mouth and all. His rotten grin persisted, but he didn't follow through. "See," he said, "Dere ya are, den."

I hadn't yet wrung all the enjoyment out of the moment, when Will, fighting for his life, yelled his final shot. "WHAT YOU DO WIT DA BABY IS YOUR PROBLEM!" and ratlike,

21

scampered off up the sidewalk, leaving me to fill in the silence, made all the more lengthy by my sudden awareness of the two open-mouthed ladies within touching distance who already had put their story together. One was certainly the type to tell, and the other one was only an old acquaintance of my mother's.

It was going to be a good day for them. They moved on. I could still see him. My childhood crush, who hadn't changed since the days of his falling socks, shrunken V-neck sweater, and his runny nose. There he is, and with his bouncing wicker lunchbox and cleated workboots and the torn comic book jutting out of his back pocket there's no mistaking the man for a boy.

It was true that my mother didn't care for the boy or the man. Didn't care for him. Didn't recognize him. Didn't want to know about him. But, what Will didn't know or wasn't interested in knowing was that my mother had felt the same about my father as a young man. Not that Dad liked to drink. He didn't have the constitution for it. But her bashful young fella from Carbonear had better make plans to come up with something better than bull labour or he'd have to start looking for someone else. He was sure of one thing, he would have some climb to her family's house. (We're still there.) She gave him one year. He did it, with a week to spare. Not the grandest job in the mill but good enough for a stiff collar and tie, which is what he featured on the evening he brought her the ring. He's gone through a lot of collars and ties since then, and I still think he looks slightly out of his element. Mom won't hear of it, unless she needs to point it up in an argument. Otherwise, he's perfect. Turned out exactly as she knew he would.

But she still gets faint when I mention Will Cole. He's beyond it, and never the twain shall meet, or even talk on the telephone.

* * * * *

I had mentioned Will's name only a few hours before he was to cinch Mom's opinion of him for ever and all time.

He had quit school and that had affected me deeply, and

22

was, I'm sure, the reason for my sudden drop to the low nineties in everything but English Lit. But no one knew more than I how important it was for Will to find a bigger playground for himself. He found it.

The last few people had come out of the theatre and were watching with the rest of us. I hadn't seen him for a while, and never like this. Will was having trouble manoeuvring, because, at sixteen, he had not yet learned to disguise his drinking. Nor did he care to.

The '51 Pontiac appearing behind him, didn't see Will for the longest time. When it looked as though it would miss him, Will seemed to stumble and stagger right back into its path. There was a long horn blast and a screech of brakes as the driver, one of the Dwyers from Botwood Road as it turned out, turned the car into the sidewalk. As it went by Will gave it a nothing glance, almost like that of a bored matador, and continued on. But Dwyer had now abandoned his car and was almost upon him. I screamed and Dwyer swung at Will at the same time. My mother wanted to go. My father sensed that I would feel like a traitor if I left, (not that I could do much more than shed the odd tear for him). So he managed to drag it out to the end.

Will got over the first blow, followed with a swing of his own, and landed on his bum in a small pool of muddy water. He got to his knees and slowly and carefully raised himself to an upright position. Someone's shout of "GIVE IT TO HIM WILL," helped a bit, but not much. Dwyer's next trick tore off the whole front of Will's shirt, and while Will was watching his falling buttons, I would have to say Dwyer got in the best one of the evening.

My mother had gone on ahead, and now my father was tugging at my sleeve. "But that's Will," I squeaked through a fresh flow of tears. "I know. I know. Maybe he's learning something tonight. Come on, sweetheart."

Before we left, I heard Dwyer say something really dirty to Will and go for his car. As he turned his back, Will, looking around for what I thought would be a wallet or something, came up with a pretty good stick. He focused on the man's retreating figure, followed for a few steps and

was about to do it, when he saw my father and me. A typic-
ally great grin invaded his bloody mouth. "HEY! HOW
ARE YA GETTIN' ON ROOT?" "Fine, Will, how are you?,"
I foolishly asked. "LOVELY, TELL YOUR MOTHER." But
I didn't after all.

He stood there, king of the empty street, like a frozen suit
of winter underwear on a December clothesline, watching
us turn the corner towards home. And all seemed at an end,
until the voices: "LOOK OUT WILL, HERE COMES THE
FORCE." "HOLY JUMPIN', SO IT IS." "YOU WAIT RIGHT
THERE, YOU LITTLE BUGGER." Then a lot of footsteps
and Will's fading but distinctive laugh, that I was to hear
again before that night was over.

On my street, no less. I don't know how long he'd been
out on the road, but I heard his very first footstep on the
verandah. Mom and Dad, must have been sleeping like logs
not to have heard it as well. I was laying out my clothes for
the next day. (The green-and-white candy-cane dress. I
always liked that dress.) In the same thirty seconds I saw
him and I was down at the front door in my stocking feet.
"Will, it's after twelve o'clock. What're you doing up here?"

I could still see a smear of dried blood in the area of his
nose and mouth. "Hello dere, Root, did I wake yer fodder?"

I was terrified to see him there on Mrs. Lowe's very own
verandah, but delighted that he walked all the way uptown
to see me.

I made him wait till I got my shoes and a raincoat and
joined him on a dark part of the street, a house or two
down.

"Well, when did you start all this?" I was referring to his
drinking.

He shrugged, and grinned, and tossed a bunch of jangled
curls out of his eyes. Besides his cockiness I saw something
else. Something I had been suspicious of all along. A desper-
ate trace of loneliness. Maybe just for me. I hoped so, as
I've always hoped so, but I still told him I had to go in.

He made me stay. He pushed his hands deep in his
pockets and tried not to stagger in place, but he did, a bit,
and I said nothing about it.

24

"Please," I said, "I don't want to be seen here like this. Let's walk."

"Sure. I bet I could walk it off."

As we walked down the shoulder of the slightly wet and shiny street he tried to look normal, and I looked as though every decent person in the world could see me.

"Root?" His whisper was dear.

"What, Will?" I sensed a difference in him and wanted to hear it all right there and then. Drunk or not, I deserved to know his true feelings about me.

"If I has to t'row up, where'll I go?"

I couldn't believe we'd walked all the way downtown and were now walking along the narrow path to the cove. Even before we climbed down to the bottom level, the bashing, swirling water in the mouth of the cove seemed almost in my very eardrums. My eyes followed the bedrock to the bottom and the main, large, flat area of coloured stones, washed smooth by the frequent high tides. The light from that enormous moon showing off the small pebble beach and the river roaring by, bringing with it the discarded logs and "nugs" from the Anglo-Newfoundland Development Company, and depositing some of them in the cove ahead of us. Tomorrow, the kids would be down here with their brin bags and pickpoles to gather up wood for the wood stoves. Will had done it, when they were able to find him and talk him into it.

"I've never been here before."

"What? Never been to da old cove?" He started down. "Come on."

The first part of it was dangerous looking, but I chose not to tell him I was a bit afraid. "Will, be careful, you've been drinking."

"Ah h-h. I could do dis on me head, girl. In fact, I did once. Da first time I tried it."

We got down all right, walked towards the cove and settled on a huge flat, yellowish rock. Will's favourite.

We surveyed his private retreat, and it meant something to me. Will stretched out almost immediately and grinned his saucy grin up at me.

"You tell lies, don't you?" I asked, to clear up a point that'd been bothering me.

"Dat's right."

"You didn't quit school because you had to help out at home, did you?"

"Nope."

I told him he should still be in school, shouldn't be drinking, and everything else I could find wrong with him. And there was a lot. In fact, when I was through, I was surprised that I found myself sitting there with such a person.

He got wise on me. "When ya starts work, da whole ting changes, see, girl. You don't know about it."

"Grand Falls is going to get too small for you soon, I guess."

"Y're nuts. I loves it here." That really surprised me. "An' I loves da mill an' ever'ting."

"It'd be even better if you'd go back to school," I said.

"No, by God. Dat's too big a price to pay for an education." He was still looking up at me with those crazy-twinkle eyes, and swinging his crossed leg because of some unexplainable built-up excitement within him. "Hey Root. Come back here. It's great, b'y."

I ignored him. But I wished I could find some other subject to talk about. This one was boring me to tears. "You don't want school, you don't want church. Do you want to be a bum?" He shot up beside me.

"I don't know, how much does it pay an hour?" and with that, he flung himself back down on the rock, laughed like a goat, and kicked his rubbery legs all over the place.

My head was suddenly full of all the terrible things he'd said to me and the embarrassment he'd put me through since I was little. The idea of lying down beside him put me in a very Uptown mood. Besides, he would have forgotten it all tomorrow. And I was right. Years later, he'd even forgotten my being at the cove with him.

* * * * *

Here's a free word of advice about Will Cole: if he ever gets too cocky with you, ask him about his birthday party years ago—and mention my name. The master plan for it was a really good one I suppose, and conceived to make the best of a dull day. If I'm not mistaken his brother Lon had been offered a truck trip to the Fox Farm, Will's favourite of all places to go. That left Will on his lonely own, so he decided to go to a birthday party. His own. He stood in the middle of Fourth Avenue and shouted out invitations to those he would most like to attend. "HEY ERIC. COME ON. I'M GOIN' TA HAVE A BIRTHDAY PARTY. HEY GEORGE! HEY TOM! HEY WALLACE!" At any other time they might have thrown rocks his way but a birthday party is different; so they gathered round, to help out in areas that were not yet quite complete. Will's demands seemed not unreasonable. "I'm goin' to make some ice cream. You get da sugar! Who'll get da cream? You get da saltpetre! Wallace, you can bring your freezer if ya wants."

All but one took off. Wallace lived next door to Will, so it might have been a little tougher to convince him. What're *you* goin' to bring?" he said, looking out of his one good lens. (The other was completely covered with adhesive tape. Someone had stepped on it.)

Will pointed out that it was *his* birthday for God's sake. He reminded the others in a very loud voice to tell their mothers that it was his birthday, and to Wallace: "If ya don't bring someting ya can't come."

Wallace was no fool. "If I don't come, you won't have a freezer."

Will can be scary at times. He held up a clenched fist. "See dat? Know what's in dere? A small spider. If ya don't bring your rotten old freezer, I'll pump this spider up wit da bicycle pump an' put 'er down yer pants an' tie yer legs togedder at the bottoms." Knowing how Wallace felt about spiders helped some.

"Go on," said Wallace, "You don't have a bicycle pump."

"I'll borrow yours," said Will, with deadly quiet.

When Wallace asked Will what he wanted for his birthday, he found out. A gun. No. Two guns and a bullet belt. A pocket knife "wit' a pearl handle." Shows him his fingerless mitts. "Mitts." A small horse. All right, wooden. Like The

27

Painted Stallion. A catapult. No, the horse doesn't need to have a saddle—but a cart would be nice, and that's all till Christmas. Wallace checked Will's fist, and was off.

With everyone taken care of, he entered his woodshed and cleaned it up. Sweeping, piling up stray kindling and coal, and putting in place a number of log ends for seats. This done, he rubbed his hand across a dripping nose and ran it down the side of his pants.

They arrived. For each present they received a "Tanks." (Will had manners.) The gifts were piled in a corner and the freezer was set up. In went Tom's sugar, George's cream and Eric's saltpetre. "Now, stir. Wallace, you want to start, like a good b'y?" A disgusted Wallace started the crank.

Will, magnanimous as always, offered to get the bowls. When asked by his mother and his eldest sister, Hilda, why he needed them, he was as cool as ever. "It's my birt'day." Then left with the bowls, and went back into the shed. "Comin' along all right, idden she?" Wallace gave him a look.

The restlessness really started when his sister Hilda arrived at the woodshed with a plate of peanut butter sandwiches, which was her attempt to right the wrong somewhat. "Where's da cake?" said Wallace, bathed in sweat. "Is dat all we gets? Peanut butter sandwiches? WHERE'S DA BIRTHDAY CAKE?"

Will should have been an actor. "Me mudder took sick dis morning. Some bad, she is. Flat on her back on da dining room table. Can't move 'er. No one knows what it is. She turned right green and couldn't finish cookin' da cake, an' it turned right rotten an' shrunk all up. Da peanut butter is some good though brudder." (Not easy in one breath.)

Well, things were tough enough but he managed to get through a pretty touchy few seconds until Wallace, with a certain amount of suspicion, slowly started up his crank again. Will must have sensed the doubt around him because he relieved Wallace at the crank and got in about three turns before we arrived on the back bridge to the wood shed. (The other part of the "we" was Maggie Pomeroy from downtown.)

I had, as usual, felt nervous and incredibly awkward on Will's street, and entering his yard and stepping up on his very own back bridge made me shake and mince my steps like a baby fawn in black bear country. I hung back a good ten paces behind my friend. (I wonder if Maggie ever knew why I gave her my old Shirley Temple doll and carriage that morning.) I waited for Maggie to knock at the palace gate, for my first look at The Potentate himself.

She did, and not tentatively either. The door opened just wide enough for us to catch a glimpse of the goings on. I would have known Prince Charming's voice anywhere. "DAT'S DAT TING FROM UPTOWN. ON MY BRIDGE. WHAT DOES SHE WANT? BOY, SHE'S SOME UGLY. UGLY! UGLY! UGLY!"

There are three things that can hurt me. Sticks and stones and names, and he knew it. I shriveled up at the tone of his voice, and Maggie's brave front didn't matter too much. Will was at the door. "WHAT D'YA WANT. WE'RE BEIN' DIRTY AN' WE DON'T WANT ANY GIRLS AROUN'."

"That's a freezer." ventured Maggie.

"YES, DAT'S A FREEZER, NOW GO HOME, YER MUDDER WANTS YA!"

A voice from inside: "IT'S HIS BIRTDAY PARTY. SO DERE. NOW GO HOME!"

I don't know how they could possibly have heard my little angel-voice from way back where I was quaking. "It can't be. His birthday and my birthday are the same. July twelfth."

At no time, in Will Cole's presence as boy or man, has it been that quiet for so long. The face at the opening in the woodshed door, changed shape. No longer was it Will's. His eyebrows curled, his nostrils flared, his little cheeks shivered and the veins in his neck did tricks, and one had to be amazed at this on-the-spot impression of Blackbeard the Pirate.

He didn't even acknowledge his guests as they filed by him with their gifts and their goodbyes. "BLOODY LITTLE LIAR!" "SOME BIRT'DAY PARTY!" "GIMME DAT, DAT'S

29

MINE!" and the last was Wallace, dragging his freezer. "I'LL BE BACK FOR DA HORSE."

It was time to go. In fact Maggie had already gone. I mouthed an apology and stepped backward off the bridge. Then having had my last look at the physical and mental wreck, hanging in midair by his nerve ends in the open woodshed door, I left.

* * * * *

He aged from that experience, and I got sick. So sick, it was worthy of the yellow-and-black QUARANTINE sign they'd nailed on the front of our house. Diptheria. And it was during this time that I discovered my mother, and learned to love her more than I ever thought possible. She became a different woman in every way: caring, tender, and completely natural for the first time in her life; and the thought that she was there, that her new-found strength was constant and ever near, was the foremost contributing factor in my recovery.

Dad's character was another, the rock base to all of us. And someone else had helped. If Mom and Dad had filled the lamp, my young Will Cole had struck the match. He had been sitting on the boulder in front of Saunders' house across the street for I don't know how long when I awoke. Fever or not, there had been through this long, long period some accompanying little nagging thought that I would be one of those people who might never be truly loved, or at least not find it for a very long time.

But was it good to see him! I watched him stand, jam his hands in his pockets, and drift back and forth between the white birches lining the side of the street. I'm sure, to some, he did look out of place among Grand Falls' better homes and gardens, but not to me. Never in my whole life to me.

I leaned out of the open window on my wobbly and knobbly legs. "HELLO."

He took his hands out of his pockets, which bulged with his ever-handy collection of glass alleys. I could see for the first time that he looked worn out. Could he have been out there all night? He tried to sound casual. "Oh—Where does

30

Bobby Delaney live?" I told him I didn't think he lived on this street. "Oh, is dat so," he said, "I used to tink he did. So long."

Doesn't sound like much of a confrontation but it put enough strength back into me to get into my taffeta dress and go downstairs. I threw my arms around my mother's neck and laughed and cried and laughed and cried and then let them put me back to bed. Weak, but happy enough to polish off an egg. That morning Dad told me how Mom, almost scared out of her wits, had insisted that she, not Dr. Strong's nurse, Theresa Maloncy, take care of me. And fearful but determined, she did just that.

The following day I got prettied up, or so my father said, and I spent most of the day downstairs. A couple of girls from my class dropped over and it was great. They reminded me that Valentine's day was only a week away. Valentine's was my day. For most kids I guess Christmas was still the big one, and it was fine; but Christmas meant more toys, and money and a lot of work, it seemed to me. But Valentine's day meant love, and I sure needed love and was thrilled to see it come around again, because I sure didn't have any left over from last year. But the little visit from Will was a good sign. Now I'd get completely recovered, and we'd pick up where we'd left off. I'd use up my whole year's collection of chocolate bar tinsel paper on only one Valentine. Will's. The others would have to go without. I'd add the tinsel to an enormous double-layered cardboard heart, edge it all around with littler hearts, and glamorize it all with the lace from two small hankies, and deliver it in person at his house.

I did, but there was no one home, so I left it between the screen door and the porch door and thought, after all, that it would probably be a lot more romantic this way.

I guess it was too bad that his brother Lon found it first but that shouldn't have mattered. And it hadn't, I thought, as I removed a smudgy envelope from our mailbox, roared up to my room, and opened it, with all the patience and gentleness that would be afforded the Dead Sea Scrolls. There it was. That was his very envelope and this was his

31

very Valentine. There were two sections, badly executed on brown paper, but nevertheless, in *two whole sections*! The question, "Would you be my Valentine?" was about to be answered.

I decided to devour the front section (the cover, you might say) and, difficult as it was, place the whole thing under my pillow and save the message for as long as I could bear to.

That was about as long as it took Mom to get supper ready. We assembled at the lace-covered table, glittering with silver and smiling family faces, and when Mom produced her roast I produced Will's Valentine.

I should have left it under my pillow. There, it had special meaning. There it had mystery, and would have given off enough love to see me through into my twelfth birthday when I could have faced it better. Anyway, "NO SIR" was what it said.

"How cruel," my mother said. "That's too bad, sweetheart," my father said. "I'm not hungry," was what I said, and I spent two days in my room, which seemed still to smell of my sickness and the fumigation that followed it.

MARY COLE

Oh, sure, she was a lovely girl. He caught me listening to him one day while he was talking to himself. Well, the stuff that came out of his mouth about that poor child. He was just shuffling around, making circles in the snow with his feet.

Bill George had just given him a haircut, so his flap cap came down to his nose and his mackinaw collar came up to his nose and he looked swallowed up.

Anyway, after school on Monday he was going to give her a smile, then walk her down over the tracks to the pipeline, being real nice to her, smiling and talking all the time and looking at her till she got all red and "Den, I'll ask her all kinds of things. Where her fodder works. Tings like dat, an' den I might even put me arm aroun' her an' take 'er down in da woods— AN' LOSE 'ER! Den she won't bodder me ever again. What am I goin' ta do wit' her anyway? The rotten little rat. Rotten arms, rotten legs, rotten ears an' rotten feet. Only ting about her dat ain't rotten is her teet'. Wonder why dat is?"

Then he marvelled for a second about the snow that fell, and having to go to school and leave it all. He loved the icicles. Snapped one off and almost broke a tooth on it. Then he followed the frost on the wires and, certainly sir, he had to test out the wire clothesline. With all the times he's seen it happen to all of us, he didn't learn a thing.

It's a terrible moment for a child, drawn by a force stronger than himself, defying every rule of common sense, daring the frost-laden wire clothesline to stick to his little pink tongue. But what's life, if not to gamble with and play in?

The moment of truth and fright and pain leaves you dangling. There are degrees of pain, really. You would just get used to standing there in silent agony and tears, when the wind would come up and jiggle the wire. This generally brought you to your tippytoes—and Will never was any good at ballet.

It was the calmest I'd ever expected to see our youngest brother, but that was not reason enough to keep him there, so I went out to help. When I got there, he had disengaged himself by slipping on the ice and was sitting there cursing the clothesline, me, Ruth Lowe, winter, Newfoundland and "King George da sixt."

Those are the absolutely only two things that Will didn't laugh about. Ruth Lowe and frosty wire clothes-lines. I'm wrong. There's one more. A certain summer wardrobe item called short pants. Especially his. Which had a button fly that opened whenever guests were coming. He blamed this condition on Harvey Hines who, it must be admitted, top-ped Will as champion Claw on the street and maybe as far as Lewisporte.

Claws aren't heard of much anymore since zippers came in, but they were something shocking to have around. The thing was, you'd be walking along—well, not if you were a girl, certainly—but someone like Will would be walking along, with his mind on some old thing, and without any warning atall, up would come a Claw, insert four fingers in the spaces between buttons and rip the whole thing open for all the world to see. Scandalous is what it was, and it generally used to happen just before they were going into school, so if they lost their buttons they'd have to wear a scribbler down in front, lashed in place by their belts.

Will's growing up was not a laughing matter. I don't mean because of Will. He was lucky to be the youngest and saw only the fun of all of it, which is something I could never get the hang of. I meant the *time* was not a laughing matter. We were poor and knew it and didn't know how to laugh. Will knew how to laugh and because of that was never poor.

* * * * *

"My son, that's shocking, you'll break Mom's heart." I was the first one he told about quitting school.

34

"Everyting goes right on t'rough. I can't pick up a ting. I'll get work an' help out." I told him he was foolish, but I couldn't think of much else to say to him. Leah was listening, and she told Hilda, who shouted the most. Not so much at Will, but more the hardness of the time, the confusion in our heads and the emptiness of the cookie jar.

Ruth Lowe told me about his trip to the principal's office. He came out of there, swinging and swaggering and grinning like a parolee from prison.

"He must have said something."

"Nuttin' wort'while."

He had already begun to form his new life in his head. He bragged about going to look for a "drop o' screech" to celebrate his freedom. She told him he was too young for that kind of thing, and he told her that he'd been doing that kind of thing for a year, now.

"If I'm old enough to slug me guts out in a paper mill, I'm old enough to drink screech." As far as the Principal was concerned: "He said, 'You didn't do too well in school.' Sure, I knew dat. I didn't need him to tell me dat."

"What else?"

" 'What're you goin' to do now?' he says."

" 'I don't know,' I says."

He told Will that other poor students had continued on, improved, and become teachers. Will told him that the only thing he would ever be able to teach would be how to get fifty per cent in Arithmetic, and that if he'd get someone else to teach the other fifty, they'd be number one. "He didn't laugh at dat."

A few years later, Ruth was to give Will a tongue-lashing that she would never again repeat for fear of losing whatever ground she had gained with him.

"You don't want to be anything better, that's the worst part. I don't know why you think it's funny and smart to get drunk and sick and fight in the streets anytime of the day or night, when decent people are going to church. I don't think it's smart. I think it's extremely dumb, and if you don't think so then I'm not your friend any more. So laugh all you want at anything you want, all your life long for all I care, and when all your rum and your brains and your youth are all gone, and you're looking around for someone's hand to hold onto, don't blame anyone but yourself if there's no one there and there's nothing left to laugh about."

But that was much later and until then he'd always been number one in the mouth department.

"Go on girl! Sure who wants ta come up to your old house, anyway? Fallin' apart, dat is. All da houses are. I wouldn't be caught dead in 'em. Sure, holy sufferin' we don't want to be seen wit you people anyway. We're all too goodlookin' down where we are."

Well, he was getting there. He'd quit school, had a drink or two, carried around his Target tobacco and papers (not hidden away down in his sock either but half hanging out of his most prominent pocket, way out front like a sign). Cleaned out Gar Morrisey's drug store of brilliantine and shaving soap and styptic pencils, and already was the veteran millworker with two shifts under his belt.

By this time all kinds of things had happened. Hilda and Leah were married. Hilda to a fine gentleman called Garfield Day, and Leah, following close behind with an uptown chap by the name of Donald Smythe, wavy haired and funny. I had a sailor, but nothing was planned. Nice though. Douglas was his name. Douglas Pope (but he never behaved like one, I'll tell you).

"There he is, the man himself." Donald said, as Will came bursting through the door and plonked down his new lunchbox with a great clatter almost enough to shatter the plates inside. Douglas asked him how he liked it and the answer was, "Fine." And was he put into the machine room?

"No. Finishin' room. Wish dey'd keep me dere. Better'n dat odder place. Still, some good to be workin'. What're ya drinkin' Donald, my son?"

Donald looked at Mom. "Can he have one of these, missus?"

"Sure I can have one," replied Will for Mom.

After Donald had poured a big one and placed it in front

of Will, Will regretted the hesitation, but with little finger akimbo, he put it away, as they say.

Lon looked as though he expected Will to bring it up in his direction so he moved off.

Will finished it, banged the glass on the table, wiped his mouth like an old sailor and squeezed out a smile—of sorts. "Well, so long for now." He gave Donald a double pat on the shoulder. "Tanks Don, my son."

Lon called him a bloody showoff, and I was the only one situated so that I could see Will's running eyes and rumpled mouth as he took off through the living room and clattered up the stairs.

I talked Douglas into playing his banjo, so it might take some degree of attention away from what I knew was coming next. And it would have, had it not been for the hot air register. As it was, there wasn't the slightest doubt in anyone's mind that the millworker was as sick as he was ever going to expect to get in all his life.

Of course at this time there had already been the war, VE and VJ days, and the boys were home. Including our brother Tom.

Will had answered the big box phone on the wall and therefore was the first to get the news and announce it to the rest of us. "We'll have to phone Hilda and Gar right away," said Leah. The cold house had been so filled with our excitement that we hardly needed our usual roaring wood and coal fire in the woodstove.

Will's own excitement was electric and lasted till Tom got home, a week from then. He wanted to be sure we knew that he was the one who answered the phone and that he was the one to tell Mom. He raced to the stairs and shouted to her. So elated that tears were in his eyes. Will, after all the awful things he had done and all the awful things that had been said about him; after all the sad and foolish people had been satisfied that they'd been there to see the worst of him, after ALL, he loved to be the bearer of good news. To be the one to touch your human heart and make you superhumanly happy.

37

"MOM, MOM, I GOT A SURPRISE," he said as she got to the middle of the stairs where she stopped. "GUESS WHAT!"

"WHAT, WILL, WHAT?"

Then he dropped his golden egg. "Tom is comin' home in next week's draft," and waited to get the full impact of her reaction, and when she lit up, so did Will. Grinning and giggling like a young fool.

"Oh—my" was about all she could say at first.

Will couldn't stress it enough. "NEXT WEEK, MOM. NEXT WEEK. DEY JUST CALLED."

"Well—well," was Mom's second, and much more explosive reaction.

Leah was on the phone to Hilda and Gar. "Next week— don't know what time—Will answered the phone, see, and you know now that he's not going to get all the information."

Then Mom really let loose. "That is grand, there's no mistake."

After Will was sure that we'd all heard and understood the great news, having told us a hundred times or more, he ran out into the street and roared around his tidings from the bottom of Grand Falls to the nearby town of Windsor.

His happiness was sincere. I could see that. But I could also see that there was despair. Relieved somewhat, but despair nonetheless. And it made him remember how it had been for him when that curious mixture of dread and patriotic excitement changed the pace of our small town life-style that was not to return for over half a decade.

*　　*　　*　　*　　*

I remember how, from the way Will was sitting, his back propped up by the woodshed, one leg on the bridge, the other hanging limply over the edge, and the tweed cap shadowing his dropping head, giving him a premature double chin, I could tell he wasn't at all interested in our pea-soup dinner, but I asked him anyway. He shifted position, but that was about all the answer he gave. He didn't want food. He wanted a uniform—any kind of uniform. A Salvation Army uniform would have done the trick.

"I'm not going to call you again," I said. I watched as he dropped his broken pearl-handled jacknife into the wood between his legs, stood, hung around the bridge for a moment more, then wandered right by the back door and down the yard toward the road.

He wandered, dispiritedly past a dozen or so houses shaped exactly like his own, stopped, and debated whether or not it would be worthwhile to re-tie his bootlace which up to then had been trailing through yesterday's rain puddles. As he bent to tie it, Sid Cater's '39 Ford came bouncing up behind him with the horn getting more of a workout than was necessary. Will, unruffled, finished, stood up and moved barely enough to let him go by. (For some reason, my brother has always had a great fancy for walking in the middle of the road.) "Dat's what dey was made for. To walk up and down on," he used to say.

His mad laugh of old had been stored away for better times, and in its place boredom took over, and the feeling that he was in the wrong time at the wrong place at the wrong age.

It was when he passed the large schoolyard with its small school (kindergarten), the large brick school (his own), and a third one (wooden), the sight of which automatically made him cross the street, that he saw it for the first time.

"For King and Country." The large white banner, lettered in red and strung from the furthermost northern window to the furthermost southern window of the grey brick courthouse, was enough to make him sick. And so were the lineups of young men in their late teens and older, who were being admitted, snail-like through the green double doors at the top of the front steps. They were like kids, going in one door to join up, and like men, coming out the other, smiling.

Will looked at them for as long as he could bear it and moved on towards the candy store. But they were there as well. Some who had already been across the street and some who had yet to go, but all celebrating their emergence

39

into manhood with the coming of the war; and all, curly heads and broad shoulders above young Will, who, as he shifted from one spot to another, looked as though he were lost among tall buildings. The chatter went on.

"What are you goin' into?"

"Navy."

"Army."

"Air Force."

"They said we'll probably leave next week."

"Here's to it."

"Good luck."

The smoke, the Haig and Moose Ales, the talking, laughing, swearing. This was where he belonged, and he thought he would smile and shoulder his way in amongst them for a cosy man-to-man, but found himself in the center of the room again, alone.

John Pond and Roland and Sid White were the next to slam their empties on the counter.

"Come on, let's get over there," said one of them and headed for the door.

"So long John," said Will. But John couldn't find who shouted, so he left.

Know what he did then? Went to the washroom, smeared the dirty burnt ends of a couple of matches across his top lip, released the snaps on his braces, lowering his short pants to just below the knee to give him the longer look (which brought his poor fly to his knees), and as rakish as you can imagine, he rejoined the others, and when the next few were ready to go, he nodded his agreement, whipped some poor man's hat off a rack as he went through the door, swooped a mangled cigarette butt off the ground, put it in his mouth, and led the march to the courthouse.

"Where the hell do ya think you're goin', my son?" says Walter Pike.

"Goin' to join up," says Will.

"How old are ya?"

"T'irty two," lowering his voice as low as his pants. Lon figured we came pretty close to getting rid of him that day.

He was put back out on the street in the most unhappy

and frustrating moment of his young life—but he stood there a long, long time instead of going home. Then he sat in the Cooperative store front a long, long time. Till the stores closed and the enlistment centre closed. He looked up and down, acquainting himself with the suddenly quiet, uninhabited Main street and broke into his grin—half joy, half mischief, but completely charming (that was to be his lifetime trademark)—at the thought that he had just inherited a town and the town would know it.

He dug from a very low pocket his old Echo mouth organ, knocked it free of old candy, chips and general dirt and dust, then played his way up and down and around and around, past tea time by the Royal Stores clock and the time when the sole of his boot came completely free, and he flapped around like a seal, and way, way past his bed time.

* * * * *

His first show of the free life was to have a lot of aggression in it; and who should find out but Jack Lowe, Ruth's father who held down a very nice job in the employment office of the mill. Mr. Lowe and I have never actually met, but he and Pop used to work together in the wood room when Lowe first came in from Carbonear and Pop and Mom came in from Trinity Bay. But of course I knew Ruth, who was what her father wanted to see my young brother about the day after his seventeenth birthday. (This was his real birthday, this was; not like the pretend one he threw in the woodshed one time. I'll have to tell you about that someday. Shocking b'y, shocking.)

Will had a very young hangover just then, so the minute he got into Mr. Lowe's office he flopped into a chair and rubbed his head.

"When did you get back?" asked Mr. Lowe.

"From where?"

"Didn't you go to the mainland?"

"No."

"Now hold on. Ruth told me you were going to Toronto. Didn't you tell her that?"

41

Will said yes, and Mr. Lowe soon found out that Will had only told his daughter that to stop her steady flow of phone calls. In other words to get Ruth off his back, you might say.

"All right. Now look here, my son. What're you playing with my daughter for?"

Will told him that he'd never played with his daughter.

"I mean causing her trouble. If you don't want to see her, that's all right. But I got an idea you're keeping her hanging."

Will laughed his awful laugh and said he wasn't keeping anyone hanging. Mr. Lowe told Will all about his friendship with our father and about how decent a fellow he was, but that Will had "the looks of a sleeveen about him."

"Who are you callin' a sleeveen." Will stood up.

Mr. Lowe made up his mind he would talk to her for Will if Will wanted, but no more keeping her hanging. "She's too good for you."

"Oh, is she?" says Will. "Listen brudder, if I t'ought she was good enough, I'd take 'er, an' nuttin' you or da ole lady could do would stop me."

He hit him. Mr. Lowe hit him. I don't swear, but Will does, and he called Mr. Lowe a bloodofabitch and told him he was going to knock his jesus head off. That was Will who said that.

Mr. Lowe put in a fast call for two men—Henry Locke and Cec Newhook, who carried him out. Will had a last word or two.

"Who wants 'er? Wouldn't touch 'er wit' a flagpole."

"She wouldn't have you," shouted Mr. Lowe.

Will told him he could take his jesus paper mill an'— The whistle blew for quitting time. Well, not really, but I'm getting tired of swearing for him.

Henry Scott's son, Andrew had been waiting outside, saw what happened and had a word with Mr. Lowe. (Andrew was a sweet boy. Will was the closest thing he had to a brother, God rest him.)

He asked Mr. Lowe if Will would be fired. "No. What's a tongue-lashing?" he said. "I've had plenty of them. Arthur,

42

his father was a gentle and sensitive man, y'know. So I expect that young fellow's got a bit of it too. He's young and he's fighting everything and everyone—and he's got other things to do than work. Well, he's right in a way. See, he's dreaming, but the mill is a fact. The mill'll always be here. After twenty or thirty years, they'll slap on a new coat of paint and douse her with oil and she'll be number one again, but we can't do that with us. We're only going around the once, and he's got to get it out of him and recognize it for what it is, because when he's a man, he'll want to remember what his childhood was all about."

If he remembers saying that last part it'll make him laugh. Because Mr. Lowe knows as well as anyone who has come within seeing distance of my brother Will, that if it was his childhood he wanted, the past would be the last place he'd ever have to look for it.

Even now, as I dump the warm loaves out on the table and watch him crossing the street and slamming the gate (and know that he's older, because I'm sure older), his manner hasn't changed a snippet since the days when Pop was alive and Hilda, Leah, Tom and Lon were living in this very house. Mom now splits up her time with Hilda, Leah, Tom, Lon and their respective husbands and wives in their respective houses, and nature has long since relieved her of the cares and struggles of our early troubled times.

But if Will's endless energy and life-style are the same, I'd have to say that his physical image can have its good and bad days. He has never consciously looked after himself, so he hasn't really kept a close eye on his body's wear and tear. Or his face, for that matter. His teeth are surprisingly good. I'm sure he must brush them, but when, for heaven's sake?

There are a dozen or so silver hairs running throughout his mop (more tangle than curl), and what used to be a dimple in his cheek is now a crease—but otherwise, he's just the same. Worse in fact.

He is, after all, a coarse man when it comes to the finer things; and yet, what had he lived for if not the finer things? A good place to board with extra quilts (that's here). A drop

43

of drink and a scattered lady friend or two. And a friend
like Andrew Scott.

*   *   *   *   *

He didn't smile when he left for work because he had
slept for four hours straight through and he's better without *any*. "But this weekend there'll be a laugh by the lovin'
God, 'cause I'm bound for hell!"

What foolishness, atall. He slammed the door, tramped
up the hallway and stopped only long enough to grab a beer
and slide his pay envelope into a pan of hot grease, making
me go in after it. And what a mess it made of my stove mitt.

"Will. You stupid thing, you!" I screamed. "What's the
matter with you?" He was already in and out of his bedroom, twice, in degrees of undress. "What's the matter wit'
you, my dear?"

" 'Tis not me, 'tis you, you foolish idiot. It's like living in
a train tunnel, being in the same house as you."

"That's no way to talk to your beautiful brudder."

"Yes, some beautiful you are, and no mistake," I said,
and started to grease the fresh loaves.

I had known about his and Andrew's trouble with Williams from the night before—since Williams's call at nine
o'clock. I only hoped Williams wouldn't be as blinding mad
when he got here as he was over the phone. Anyway, I'd
better get ready to lie again.

Will was standing in the middle of the kitchen floor,
doing a half-naked jig, with the mill dirt from the elbows
down and from the neck up—leaving the rest of his body
as white as my apron.

"You're jigglin'," I teased as he bounced up and down.

"WHO'S JIGGLIN'? WHO?" he snapped, stretching from
the waist to add extra tautness to the fat on his top half
while continuing his dance with the bottom half.

Just as he was about to lose his jockey shorts, he saw
Williams at the front fence trying to peer into the house.

"Here comes da Force!" and he hustled me down the hallway as he slipped into his bedroom.

"Tell 'im I'm out! Tell 'im I'm out!"

"I know. All right." I said, getting fed up with this whole ritual.

While I was ad-libbing for him at the front fence, Will had left his door open just enough to see clear through the house to where we were chatting. He held his trousers in front of him, ready to jump at a moment's notice but afraid to move, and muttering, "Get out of dere, ya fat—go on—ya ugly old bastard, get out. Give 'im da boot Mary. Get 'im out. Go on!"

He was momentarily distracted by his one and only bit of wall decoration. Actually it was taped to the inside of his closet door. A picture of a girl. No ordinary girl either, and not the kind of girl you might associate with Will. You know whose picture it was? Do you know? That movie star —English—Deborah Kerr. Now who would figure *that*?

That's not to say that Will couldn't get a nice girl. I'm not saying that atall. He can be a very surprising fellow if he puts his mind to it. Charming, clever, witty, dry (my, can he be dry), and oddly enough, intelligent. Yes, by heavens, even that, and if a girl could get a comb through his hair and a tie around his neck, she'd have something good enough to take inside any house in Grand Falls; or, yes, anywhere in Newfoundland for that matter. I won't venture a broader statement than that because I'm doubtful whether or not they'd know what to do with him in the Boston states or in the better homes of Georgia or the hallowed halls of England, Will being as strange (no, different) and extraordinary a fellow as he is; but if Deborah Kerr wanted a good looking, lively and standoutish kind of gentleman to grace her arm on the way to church, she'd never find a better. Mind you, she'd have to calm him down a bit with a needle or something first, because as he is now he's just as likely to throw her down in the bushes on Scotsman's hill in her new Easter outfit as look at her.

Williams had told me that after a short nap, due to the "track and field" he had to do with Will, he went out on the town in search of him, and it seemed that a lot of people had seen the boys (Andrew was with him apparently), but no one seemed to know where they were going to light for the night. I told him he didn't come home, which he was clever enough to have thought out for himself. The only other person who helped Williams out apparently was Alf Morrow who claimed they drove through his fence with Andrew's brother Cec's truck. Well, it makes perfectly good common sense to me that the man who owned the truck would be the man to go and see. But it was dark, the truck lights were on, shining straight at the house no doubt, and if Alf Morrow is not blind as old Ned Moss, I'm Princess Margaret Rose. No one likes Alf Morrow, I told Williams, and when you don't like a man, the next logical step must be to mistrust him.

Who was next? Oh yes, Nish Perry, the man who owns the house that Will was supposed to have destroyed. Ignatius Perry. Old Nobby Perry. Now if you want to come face to face with a man who's going to hell, there he is. Don't you read the papers, Williams? or listen to the news? Nobby Perry is that sweetheart of a gentleman who was suspected of tampering with the kids' apples last Hallowe'en. How is it you can believe a reprobate the likes of him? Sure, you'd believe anything, if you'd believe that man. I wouldn't give him the pan scrapings off the cake that fell while I've been standing out here talking to you, Constable Williams, sir. His daughter can't stand the sight of him, and I don't know if you're going to locate the man who doesn't hate him.

Him and that fool—that Justin Roberts. That's another one that needs to be horsewhipped. Will kicked him, you say? Well, anyone has got a reason to kick him. Marie would be his second wife, you know. Oh yes, he's been married before. Know where she is now, or do you care? All right then. Stop trying to get away. You're rude, you are. Now, he married the prettiest thing from Bonne Bay you'd ever want to see. Pure as the driven snow. He wed her, plonked her in a drafty old house on Botwood Road, left two lovely looking children with her and ran out. That's the God's truth, and hasn't put a nickle in the mail in a month. That's Justin Roberts for you, thank you very much. You won't catch Will Cole doing that. (You won't, because

46

you won't catch him married, is what I was sorely tempted to say.)

So who are the rest of the complainants, anyone I know about? Don't be cheeky with me. Anyone I *don't* know about? My, you're getting rude. I've heard quite enough from you for this morning, and I must say you've put me in a lovely mood for the rest of the day.

I left him, just as his finger was coming up to my face for a further word, and stopped to pick a couple of forget-me-nots and went inside where his lordship called me into his room, and while I collected his dirty clothes from every corner of the room, I told him how it went.

"I'm gettin' bloody tired of dat."

"You're getting tired? Never mind, one of these days, you're going to slow down just long enough for him to get his hands on you and you'll be in that jail till it falls apart."

"Not atall. Old Williams an' me got an understanding."

"Oh you think so, do you? You don't think he's easy because he was a friend of Pop's? Anyway, off you go."

"Off I go where?"

"To St. John's. It's about that time, isn't it?"

"Tryin' to get rid of me, are ya?"

"One of these days, they're going to get fed up with you, taking time off whenever you like, and there won't be a job waiting for you when you get back. Either that or they'll shove you back down in the sulphur room, and wouldn't that be lovely? Why do you go there so often anyway?"

"Where? The sulphur room?"

"No, you blooming idiot, St. John's."

"Just a trip. A feller like me has got to get out and around now and again. Have a laugh."

As if he hasn't laughed enough. He pointed to his pay envelope tucked in my apron to remind me of his sense of responsibility. And it did remind me. He's never let me down in that department, I'll say that for him; but a good time every night of his life, as if he would crumble to dust if he stayed home once in a while, or put on a clean shirt and tie and went to church. He pretended to throw up on my display of fresh bread.

47

"All right, don't go to church, but don't keep going in circles either. Just once. Walk up the street—looking responsible, so that someone might say: "Will Cole is coming, and he's clean!"

"Hey Mary, dat'd be a lot of fun!"

"That's foolish. You're foolish. It's wrong, wrong, wrong!"

"And I s'pose Walt Little, wit' his fat gut an' his fat wife an' kids, an' the bad heart trouble, an' the payments on dat shitty looking house up in da development an' da misery written all over his face is right, right, right? You know how old Walt Little is? A good two years younger den me, an' he looks ten years older. Idden dat right?"

"Yes, but all I'm saying is there's more to life than fun!"

"Who told you dat, my dear?" He flushed down the last half of a bottle of beer, and just when I thought he'd gone, he grabbed me.

"Now, give us a kiss, ya mad sexy ting!"

Well, he tickled and slobbered and swung me all over, then left me, holding onto my jumping heart and sitting on a flattened loaf of bread, listening to his laughter echoing down the street.

I barely had the breath left for the two phone calls that followed. One from Tom's wife, Doreen, who wanted me to go to bingo with her that night, and the other from Lon's wife, Hope, who just wanted to tell me she was pregnant again. All very nice, but I was too tired out to take anything in.

And then, my brassiere strap broke. My lord, wasn't the day ever going to end?

CONSTABLE WILLIAMS

They say I don't have a sense of humour. Well, godammit, there's nothing funny about chasing a fellow off a cliff. Now, I can enjoy a good joke now and again—off duty, but do you see anything funny about running a fellow off a cliff? I don't. No, by God.

Oh, I'm not saying he meant to do it. That'd be pretty harsh. I'm not even sayin' that he enjoyed it when it happened, but I've seen him laugh about it since—laugh, for God's sake. And the more he tells the story, the more fun he gets out of it. He told it one time when I was there, and everyone laughed but me. It's not that I can't enjoy a good story, but I didn't think it was right to laugh somehow, even if it was funny, and it wasn't—but there was Will, splittin' a gut, and how a fellow can watch that and not have nightmares is beyond me.

What was curious is how the fellow didn't see the edge before he went over it. But, y'see, part of the reason it happened was that the bushes led almost right up to the edge, see, and they were thick enough not to be able to see through, and the boy—Joe Maidment's young fellow, Junior, it was—thought he had about a half-mile to go, but it was more like two feet; with Will, just a boy himself, coming after, banging away with a toy gun, see, so if Will had been just a bit closer, he would have gone over too, most likely. (I've thought about it since.)

As it was, Junior went over the cliff. Broke through the alder bushes and went over the cliff. The poor young bugger.

And didn't he fly. He must have been travellin' 'cause he went straight out and straight down, and all the scratchin' and grabbin' in the world didn't get him a small tree to cling onto. Poor young bugger.

'Course, Will got some fright too. Well, just imagine, watchin' a fellow, all arms and legs go over a cliff. An' seein' his boot come off.

Oh, that's right, I almost forgot. His boot come off, and here's something for Ripley. After the boot come off, it lodged on a ledge just a few feet down. So the boot was sove, but poor buddy kept right on goin' and—SLOWSELL!

He's okay now, y'know. Outside of a few scars you'd never know the fellow went over a cliff, an' he don't talk about it; but Will talks about it, I'll tell ya—and laughs too. Now, how in the name of God can you laugh at something the likes of that? I must mention the *Titanic* to him one of these days.

*   *   *   *   *

I knew Arthur, his father, and that's why I went to his funeral. Will was eleven or twelve, I just forget.

The coffin had been laid across the dining room table, and Billy Flood, Tommy Janes and a few other buddies of Arthur's were there for a good part of the day. If you could call any part of that day good. And there was me, and the family of course—and, if I'm not mistaken, Andrew Scott was hanging around there too and had been waiting for Will.

Will came down the stairs, having just woke up. He had seen the coffin before so he just wandered around looking at the visitors, studying their attitudes.

This must have been the slowest day in his life, and not a usual day either—seeing Lon, Tom, Hilda, Mary, Leah, and his Mom cry for the first time in his presence.

But *he* didn't. I don't know why. It was a sad enough time for him, I'm sure, but I didn't see him cry. In fact, you know what he did? I was sitting with a cup of tea on my lap. Now, I'd seen young Will around, of course, but didn't have much more than Hello to say to him—and I didn't speak to him this day, if I remember rightly; but as I was sitting there with my tea, and the rest of his family were weeping, that young fella came up to me, and the tiniest smile broke out on his face. Not a disrespectful or a nasty smile, certainly not, but a sweet little smile, I suppose you could say.

Know why he did it? He was trying to get me to smile too. Imagine that. He somehow felt it was wrong to sit moping around a coffin when the fella inside the coffin had no way of knowing if you were laughing, crying, or fixing the roof. I couldn't see the sense in that kind of thinking, so I'm afraid I glowered at him a little bit, which meant nothing to him one way or the other. But isn't that something? He *smiled* at me.

He couldn't get anyone to return his smile, so he got himself and Andrew a slice of molasses bread and they sat out on the back steps and ate it.

I thought about him a lot that day, watching him come and go. Who was going to tell him about dying? Hey? Where does he belong who likes to laugh? Who the hell could tell that funny little fella what sadness is all about? Not the family, certainly; Lon, half hidden on the stairs, his mother pressing black dresses on the kitchen table. The girls—and Tom. Each person's private grief removed from all the others.

He was left to feel the death in his own special way, and told not to interrupt the sorrow with chatter and demands for food.

Breakfast is over, young fellow—and it's too late to mend your pants. Between the tears, there's much to do before tea time.

I had a feeling, he was thinking back to his father. He wasn't like a friend that had gone away—or a wooden whistle split in two.

What kind of hurt is this for a boy? And since he couldn't get anyone to smile away a moment of this endless day, he'd stand over by Arthur's "Smoke and Be Happy" pipe-rack, and not say one word more. He'd wait till everything was done. Till someone started to sing again and smile at him again.

The front porch was too small to make the corners comfortably with the casket, so it was necessary for us to open the window and get it out that way; and when we had it situated in the hearse, and the two other vehicles were ready to roll (with the rest of us jammed in tight), young

Will and Andrew were left standing in the yard. I rolled down the window to hear what he was saying.

"Is dere room in the car for me?"

What happened then was I gave him my seat and young Andrew Scott and I went fishing, and—I never allowed myself to get any softer than that. As it happened I'm glad I didn't. With what I had to deal with in the years that followed, thank the good Lord I was in shape and could keep up with the devil.

* * * * *

"What did you do wit' your first-aid box?" He made me lose my place on the charge pad.

"Up there somewhere. Here! Empty your pockets on the desk here."

Will plastered up his cut elbow, Just a sample of what he was going to get if he didn't do as I told him.

"I haven't got anyting," he said.

"Right there! Empty 'em!"

"Just me cigarettes an' you're not gettin' dem. Dere'd be none left by mornin'."

"Tightwad."

Andrew Scott came in then and the shiftiness began. I had all I could do to keep them both in my sights at the one time—and when they got tired of trying to get behind me, one or the other of them would jump up and down or some other stupid thing to try and distract me.

"Give me your belt," I said to Will.

"No!"

"All right, down you go." I was too tired to argue any more.

"Let him go. He's on the midnight shift," said Andrew.

That made two lying bastards. He was on at eight in the morning and he wasn't even going to make that.

"I'll be dere," said Will.

"Down you go!"

Then he mocked me. "Down ya go. Down ya go. Dat all ya know?"

Andrew stalled me again by mentioning that he saw

Ruth Lowe outside. I said that I saw her too. "I did, god-dammit! Jack Lowe's girl. Sure, I know her."

"You know her," said Will, "Yer lucky enough to know how to tell da time, ya fat, ignorant ting."

"Who the hell are you calling fat? Where?"

Well, I took my eyes off him for a half a second and that sleeveen jabbed me in the gut with two hard fingers and took off through the door with the other one behind him, and they were gone for the night.

So was I gone for the night. I'd had plenty for one day, they could go to the hell's flames, the pair of them; which is probably where they'd end up before the night was out. And the thing was that what started out as a little bit of shit-disturbing, pardon my French, sometimes turned out something quite a bit different. The reason for that being that Will never knew how to govern his energies. There were times when folks were just not prepared to go all the way with him, or the time was simply not the right time, and he couldn't understand those kind of people, like Mrs. Lowe, Ruth's mother, for instance.

Will always pretended that the Uptown-Downtown idea was the reason that Ruth Lowe's mother wouldn't have him in the house. Well, that was only half true. I could go along with it, if it was the whole reason, because I wouldn't let him in my house either. All he'd need would be five minutes and I'd have to write it off as a loss.

The other half of the reason goes like this. Mrs. Lowe had been having a bad time with her nerves. I suppose it would be all right to call it a breakdown. She'd been that way since she'd lost her only sister.

I never cared much for jannying or mummering or dres-sing up or whatever the hell it was. I never did it myself, and it just created another big bloody nuisance for the force. Especially when you got Will Cole and Andrew Scott out roamin' free on the town with their heads full of home brew. They're bad enough when you can see where they are, but when they got dressed up in the sheets and the caps and the bloody big fisherman's boots and the lot, you might as well try to find Billy House's pig in Buckingham Palace.

But the call came in and I was on my way. Apparently, these two jannies showed up at the Lowe's house. When Ruth first opened the door she thought they were children, because the boys were on their knees.

They both had the big sheets on and old salt and pepper caps on top of that. That'd scare the jesus out of anyone. Will figured she'd spot his voice right away so Andrew did the talking (in a high voice) while Will gummed away on the mouth organ. (He also had a jew's-harp for variety.)

Her father was putting in a little overtime at the mill, leaving her in charge of her mother, who had had enough of lying in bed and was cosily set up alongside the fire, sipping ginger ale. The house had been as quiet as heaven before the doorbell rang.

"Who is it Ruth?" she called to her daughter. "Two jannies—Listen."

She had Will play a little louder for her mother's benefit. Her mother smiled. How quaint.

"They want to come in and dance for us," called Ruth.

"No. Give them a nice glass of syrup and tell them, not tonight."

Isn't that sweet, Ruth's mother must have thought. Was it Janny Night already? She rested her head on the wing of the large brocade-covered chair and remembered a Janny Night of quite a few years before when, reluctantly, she had agreed to make the rounds with friends from her class. She supplied the sheets. They'd brought the caps and boots and all of that. So, gathering at her house, they had all (about six of them) had a glass of raspberry syrup apiece, then passed around the boots, caps, musical instruments, and the whole pile of them had got under the sheets.

They only got to one house before someone guessed who she was, so that meant she had to lift her sheet and be herself for the rest of her visit. And there happened to be another janny there, not from her group, who sat silently in the corner for the longest time, drinking a glass of screech. She had an idea that it would have to be Jack, who had just arrived from Carbonear and who she'd met just once before.

While the others were playing their songs and dancing their jigs, she kept her eye on this other one. She was positive it was Jack, and having had a sip of screech herself she boldly slipped from one spot to another until she was standing next to him. When he spoke to her, without revealing his identity, she was sure it was him, and since there were no more chairs and he'd offered his knee for her to sit on, she blushed, but accepted.

Now, apparently this janny had been making the rounds for years and not once had anyone guessed him—till this night. After Ruth's mother had been sitting on his knee for a good half-hour. There never was a plainer man than "Red" Hunt and never would be again.

That was her one and only Janny Night, and as quaint as the custom was, she's never, ever let them in her house.

It has to be said that it was Ruth who let them in. "Hello darlin'. Would you like a song or a jig?" This time it was Will, but she still didn't recognize him.

Their high shrieky voices and snickers brought, "Who are they dear?" from the inside room. Between giggles, she told them they had to go.

"We'll do it for nuttin', if you'll let us in," said Will.

"Oh please, a tiny slice of old Christmas cake and a glass of strawberry syrup, like yer mudder says."

"Well, all right, but—"

"Good enough," shouts Will in his normal voice and the two of them stand and pound past Ruth, down the hallway, and with sheets flying the two terrible looking sights made themselves at home.

"Hello dere Missus," said Will, swaggering up to Mrs. Lowe's chair and almost scaring her to death.

"Oh no. You have to leave," she said.

"Oh no. We have to stay," said Will.

"If I say you'll leave, you'll leave. Now go. This very minute. I'm not well."

"Oh Jesus, no. No one's sick on a night like dis. We'll fix

55

ya up real good. Just hold on now till I gets me sheets squared away."

He gathered up his sheet, banged away on his mouth organ, starting off with "The Exploits River Whore," and almost tearing the floor boards up with the stomp of his foot.

Andrew wasn't any different, except he had Will's jew's-harp and he couldn't play it.

Well, they roared up the stairway and down again, in through the kitchen, up across her cupboards, slam-bang again on the floor, jiggling china cabinets, drumming the table tops, pulling each other's sheets, stumbling, tumbling and looking for liquor.

Poor Mrs. Lowe had no voice left and all Ruth could seem to do was point to the door, which made about as much impression as a nipper's bite on an elephant's arse, excuse my French.

"I s'pose we'll have to drink our own, Andrew old man." Will came up with a half-empty bottle of something or other from a back pocket and they passed it back and forth. "Have a little bit Missus. Good for ya. What've ya got, woman's troubles. Hee-hee-hee-e-e."

By now Mrs. Lowe had very stiffly propped herself up in a corner. Her eyes very much afraid. And she was holding a poker in front of her, not quite ready to strike, if she needed to.

"You're bothering my mother. Now stop it. Stop it!" shouted poor little Ruth, pulling on their sheets. But Will was too high to hear. As I mentioned before, when he got like this he figured the whole world loved him and he was oblivious to all else.

Here, he grabbed Ruth and started swinging her around to Mrs. Lowe's absolute horror. Andrew had picked up the mouth organ and was giving them a rousing good "chin" dance. Will spread Ruth's arms wide and wheeled her speechless, although, if you looked closely you'd see that along with being sort of terrified, she wasn't doing it totally against her will, and Mrs. Lowe saw this.

"Stop it, Ruth. Stop it." But she couldn't be heard above the din, so she came out swinging her poker, until she was heard. "Get away from her, get away. Stop laughing, Ruth, stop. Stop."

"Please, Will, please let me go." Ruth pulled away from him and went to her mother, who was now shaking from weakness.

"What's the matter wit' her?" says Will, spilling screech all down his front and into his long rolled-up hip-waders. And then to Andrew—"Come on, my son. Onward. Let's get the jesus out of here!" Then: "See ya, Root!" as though not a thing had happened—and knowing Will's thinking, nothing had.

"Don't cry. They've gone."

"Savages. Savages. And you—danced and laughed. You forgot everything I taught you. Everything." Then she slapped her. "Why did you laugh?"

"I just thought—a little fun—even their kind of fun for a change. I thought a little laughter in my life would be good for me."

But she certainly wasn't going to find too much with Will Cole. It's not that he didn't care for people, and it's not that he didn't know his friends from his enemies, because once they showed their colours and Will stopped long enough to recognize them, that was it then and you knew it, and there was no way it could ever be changed back.

There probably was a time when those two could have matched up pretty well together I suppose. Who could tell? For the amount of time it would take her to get him all figured out and to wait till he grew up and calmed down, it mightn't be worth it.

I don't know though. I'm sure there are those who have spent their lives on worse things than people, and again, it would be a matter of catching him in between. What I mean by that is she would have had to be around when he'd stopped long enough to allow the bigger, more important world to show him just how small a part of it he was. (Never in his lifetime, but she'd have to find that out

57

for herself.) At a funeral, perhaps, when it was someone else's day (that'd be the day!), or—or—I don't know—when he was taking a pee. How would I know these things?

* * * * *

There was one such a pause in his life. I had just bought a new pair of sneaker boots at the Royal Stores and, although they looked good from the outside, my low arches on the inside were getting one hell of a going over, so I was only good for one or two half-assed innings of cricket before I gave it up as a bad job and curled up on the grass.

The Lowes were out at the Fox Farm that day. Now, why was it I always thought of Mrs. Lowe as being stuck up? She's the nicest kind of lady, and after offering me a second plate of their beet salad, I told her so.

I was about to ask where Ruth was when she appeared at the trees and came running towards us with two other girls her age: Rita, I forget her last name, and Alice Cooke, Norm's daughter.

Mrs. Lowe asked Rita (what the hell's flames is her name?) how her mother was.

"Fine," said Rita. "They're down at the other end."

"Oh good. Jack," she said to Ruth's father, "Jack, we'll have to drop down and see them before we leave."

Jack Lowe, God bless his soul, refilled my cup with a drop of his own beer. Well worked off too, I thought, and I mentioned it to him.

The other girl had not been spoken to, as yet. "Mom, you know Alice Cooke," said Ruth.

"You're not Viola's girl?" asked Mrs. Lowe.

She was Viola's girl. I knew it right away, and so did Jack.

"'Course she is," he said, "and Ralph is her brother."

"Yes," said Alice. "Ralph was killed last week. Crashed in the Atlantic, on his way to Africa."

The very names of those places were strange to her, but the sweet little thing was as brave as she could be, and I mentioned it to Jack, after.

But it was a pretty shocking moment, let me tell you,

and Mrs. Lowe took it all very decently. "My goodness, Alice, we didn't know a thing about it."

"That's right. How awful," said Jack.

"How awful, is right," I said.

"I guess not too many people would know. Ever since we moved to Windsor, we don't spend much time in Grand Falls."

"That would be it," I said.

Ruth took three apples out of a basket and gave one to each of the girls.

"Here. Let's go."

Mrs. Lowe offered them some of the real nice ham but they turned it down.

"Give our best to your mother, Alice."

"All the best," I shouted, and allowed my empty cup to fall over. Do you know that in jig time Jack had it straightened up and filled to the brim.

"Poor Viola. We went to school together in Corner Brook. Poor Viola." Mrs. Lowe wiped away a sincere tear.

It couldn't be any more than ten minutes when young Will Cole arrived. His head looked as though it had been dunked in a barrel of brilliantine, his V-neck sweater had an elbow out, his shoes weren't shined, and his pants were baggy at the knees, but still, somehow—no, he wasn't my idea of the model sixteen-year-old boy from lovely Grand Falls. Nor was he up to any good, as he carved a path through the tall grass at the edge of the trees. A pup on the loose for other young pups.

Before long, Ruth, who mustn't have brought her brains with her that day, had latched onto him. But still, I suppose you could say that he was paying her a decent amount of attention, and as I sipped my cup of beer and watched them weaving in and out of the small trees and bobbing in and out of my vision, it reminded me of my young constable days.

They landed, finally, still unbeknownst to her parents. Winded and laughing as they were, they looked pretty good together, I must say that.

And then, the welcome and most eagerly and patiently

59

awaited train whistle. Not just the usual blast either, but that day's whistle seemed to have a special sound to it, and it tooted and tooted, for all the world to hear, its happy song.

All at once, our fieldful of people rose up in a sitting position. We must have looked like ducks in a shooting gallery, or squirrels jerking up at the sound of man. But this was it, and no mistake. The field was completely abandoned in a matter of seconds and, strange as it seemed to me, Will was the first to leave. I say strange, because I knew what he had gone through when the boys went away.

Ruth ran after him, and her parents were still too busy to see that they might have lost a daughter and gained a real problem that very afternoon. Those of us who watched and waited for that damned slow thing to pull into the station were on the edge of a joyful hysteria, and after it was sighted coming around that last bend, full to the brim with our grand heroic boys, it was as if we were all wired together and plugged into the same outlet and, when it finally lumbered in, I was sure we were.

The crowd of us, who during the waiting had resembled an enormous family portrait, were now coming apart like a shattered jigsaw puzzle. For here they were, and there was the long canvas banner, stretched from the front to the caboose, which told us so: THE ROYAL NEWFOUND-LAND REGIMENT.

I spotted Will and Ruth who, like myself, were being jolted, jostled, and practically carried to the train by the cheering crowd, and by now we could even identify some of the faces of the boys as they shoved and pulled for position at the train windows.

Will was shouting like the rest. Perhaps even louder, but along with the curiosity and excitement, his face was registering a terrible sadness. I saw Ruth shoulder her way through to be closer to him. There's no doubt about it, his adventure had been stolen from him and lived by others.

So for a second there, early that afternoon, they seemed to fit, but after that, I could have told her that she'd never have the chance again.

I threw my keys on the desk, and had a look at my old face in the mirror. Will and Andrew had been out there on the town, gallavanting around, causing problems for other people; and for the very good reason that there had been *seventy-five* hours to that day, I thought I'd collapse on my night-duty cot and turn into the wall. Which I lost no time in doing.

ANDREW SCOTT

Mary guessed right: Will would be on his way to St. John's again, but first he had to get through the next day's shift and rid himself of the worst hangover since yesterday morning's—helped out a bit by taking his lunch up on the roof of the mill. But not helped by the fact that he and I and Barry Rose and a few others, whose company he could manage, were joined by our machine tender, Walter Little (who wasn't manageable and who didn't include Will Cole as one of his favourites of all-time good fellows).

There were one or two others down along the roof, who moved their boxes up to add to our little group.

Will liked it up here. Even with a hangover. The new machine which this enormous building housed was called "Moby Dick" and the roof was just long enough, wide enough, and uncluttered enough to provide Will with the kind of domain a squire like him should have.

Barry Rose arrived with our lunches and handed Will the sweater he'd asked him to get. Walt Little and two others were sitting in a row along one bench, which seemed right somehow, because they all seemed to suit each other, and although they were all about the same age as Will, they looked a lot older. Older, paunchier, and taking it all out on Will.

"Go on, you and Will didn't finish school together, did ya?" asked Frank Downs, a haunted, caved-in looking man with one big eyebrow.

Walt was eager to say that Will never finished at all. "I went on an' graduated but Will quit a few years before. Up to then, we were in the same class. Weren't we, Will?"

"True."

"You shoulda finished, Will," said Walt. Then swigged his milk and dripped it all over himself and Frank Downs' right knee. Frank didn't notice.

Will asked why he should have finished, and Walt pointed out that it would have been worth it for the bigger pay envelope: the bigger job, the bigger house, and the wife "waiting for ya in 'er bath robe."

"Walt," said Frank, "tell Will and Andrew what you told me—you know, about yesterday."

Walt laughed and coughed for a while and finally got it out. "I come in the house—now listen to this. I said 'Let's go to bed.' She said 'No.' An' I said 'Never mind your NO, GET 'EM DOWN.' An' by Jesus, she did."

"That all?" said Will, sprinkling salt, very daintily on his potato.

"Yeah."

"Dat's pretty funny Walt," said Will.

"An' it's free y'know. You can't get much better than that."

"No, not much better," said Will, who up to now hadn't even promised to look into Walt's face.

Frank got annoyed with Will for no reason at all. 'Course Will annoyed Frank on sight. If he only passed him on the street, Frank would automatically begin to frown and massage his gut in his ulcer region.

Frank was disgustingly married. "Now come on Will, you can't tell me you wouldn't get married if it was given to you." By now, he was practically shouting. "Why don't you get married for Jesus' sake?"

In a much less aggressive tone, Will told him that if he did get married, Frank and his missus would probably have Will and his missus over for a feed of pork and cabbage and a game of cards, and "dis way, dere's not much chance of dat, see Frank."

Frank's big eyebrow moved up and down, but he said nothing until he'd thought it out.

"Well, 'tis your life I s'pose," said Walt, grudgingly.

Frank had thought it out. "I know that I wouldn't know what to do without the wife and kids."

Will was having a whale of a time and judging by his sly twinkles in my direction, he was putting his act together. So I helped.

"How many you got now Frank?" I asked.

Frank didn't answer immediately. His bottom lip drooped,

and with a note of slight disbelief in his foggy voice he said "Nine," in a weak mumble.

"How many?" I asked.

"Nine," he hollered. "An' I wouldn't give 'em up for anything." (Unless perhaps you offered him a stick of gum or a balloon.)

Without turning his head, Will took in the benchful of aging young men. I had to turn away so I wouldn't spit out my fishcake.

Well, that fellow can come up with an unexpected turn of phrase. Maybe he pulled it from behind his ear with his half-smoked cigarette. He lit it.

"You see—the ting is—I'm a hedonist . . . you know, Walt?—Well, I mean—dere's more to epicureanism than a good meal—hey Walt? Hey? Walt? Hey?"

During this he had patted Walt's paunch as if he were dribbling a basketball.

I was delighted. Where'd he learn that, I wondered. Frank nodded repeatedly, pretending that Will was speaking his language, but Walt stared straight through him.

"How would you like a punch in the chops?"

"What's da matter," said Will, not quite pulling off his amazed expression.

"You know goddamn well what's the matter. I don't like lookin' foolish."

"Ya'd never know it to look at ya," said Will.

Walt was standing by now and ready to tear the roof apart.

Frank, whose idea of fighting was punching his pillow, tried to get Walt into a hand of cards instead.

"Don't worry," said Walt. "I wouldn't hit him. If I did, there'd be nothing left of him. Look at him, for Christ'sake. Grinnin' like a goddamn monkey. Same as he was in school —an' just as childish. He's not married because he ain't grown up enough to get a good woman."

Walt was never very good at forecasting the weather, so he didn't see the storm coming up in Will.

"And," he continued, "if he ever did, she'd prob'ly be some old whore. That's all that would have 'im."

I didn't know whether to laugh or cry. When my friend lowered his head, he was still grinning. Then there was a terrific rumbling starting up within him and creating what was to be the god-awfullest, belt snapping, throat-bursting roar, and when he raised his head and looked to the sky, there had been a total transformation that had even me wondering for a second if he'd gone funny on me.

While still in his roar (without drawing a breath), Will gripped the big wooden cable-reel that held our lunch boxes and brought his hands straight on up, tipping this bloody great thing over onto the lot of them. Then (they were scampering backwards), Frank tripped on a loose boot lace and four-footed his way across the cinders to the ladder, where, he later discovered, he'd worn out both knees.

"I'll kill him. That'll stop him," shouted Walt who, despite this, managed to get to the ladder before Frank.

Following the cable trick, the air had been filled with their flying lunch boxes. All except mine (which I wouldn't give to Will, even though he'd asked for it) and Will's own, and Barry Rose's, who Will liked a lot.

The silence that followed seemed unreal. Then—the starting whistle.

"If he comes back, I'm in the toilet," I said, and left the roof.

"I always knew they'd come and get you someday brother," said Barry, and he left too.

"Didn't dey go?" said Will, back to normal now. "Who's for a beer after work? You old enough to get into Henry's yet?"

"No," said Barry, "Besides, I've got to go bowling."

"Bowlin'?" shouted my friend, as Barry had started his climb down the ladder.

"Jesus. Bowlin'. Don't get into any trouble."

Alone with the quiet and the overturned reel and the litter from five or six lunches. Some wet, some dry. On the peak of the roof, turning to face all directions, he'd put you in the mind of one of them ancient explorers who was figuring out what next to discover. He picked up an overturned bench, laid it right side up, stretched out on it, with his hands behind his sweaty head, and chuckled. "King of da Castle." And I would give him that.

*   *   *   *   *

The only reasons people went to St. John's when we were kids, I remember, were to see a specialist (if Dr. Strong and Dr. Brown couldn't handle it) or to the nut house, or the reform school or the pen, or for your Christmas liquor. No, you could order *that* from your house (to add to the home brew that you'd make yourself).

It's funny about that. Will was always content enough just kicking up dust in this old town; then he had to go to St. John's—oh, about three years ago, to have something looked after, and hasn't stopped going back. About every two or three weeks or so.

I wonder if he'd mind my telling you what he had to have looked after. Oh, hell, I don't care if he does. There would never have been any reason to mention it atall except for Alec Lodge, who spread it around the mill that he was going there for a *sociable disease*. (Not to get one, to have one looked after.) Now anyone who knows Will would know that he'd never hide a thing like that. Not only would he get it fixed right here, but he'd probably tell you about it himself and throw in the name of the girl as well. (He was pretty honourable with the women, as far as their various identities were concerned, but not when it came to the sociables. Then it was every man and woman for himself.)

Anyway, you'll gather by now that it wasn't for anything like that. But the truth was that Alec was not far off. Well, let's say his geography was right. (Maybe I shouldn't tell it. Yes, by God, I will.)

He froze it! Now how about that for pleasure? Well, laugh? I thought my pants would never dry. To Will, that's like being a house-painter and someone taking his brush away.

A young fellow from the States had been moose hunting and got lost between here and Gander Lake. Will and me joined a group of volunteers to go and get him. Well, it was

67

one godawful time to get lost, I'll tell you. Worst winter in twenty years and not too well organized, the whole thing.

Anyway, I could only stay out for about a day, but his majesty stuck it for close to a week. Well, he got clear of his group somehow and went a little bit too far astray (he thinks he's a good man in the woods and he's not, unless he's got a woman to lead the way), and he missed meeting his truck at the rendezvous point. They came on without him, leaving word with the next group that Will hadn't shown up, but that he shouldn't be too hard to find. And they were right, he finally stumbled upon the marked fir trees again and wound up out on the road, in time to meet the next truck, which was the last truck, before they gave up the search.

Fine. Except for one thing. They had found the Yank, frost bitten and everything, but alive, and piled him into the only possible space that Will could've occupied on his way back.

There was one hell of a lot of cursing and swearing and bad feelings in that bitter bloody evening, I can tell you. The owner and driver of the truck was a fellow by the name of Walt Little, Will's friend from the mill roof.

"Look buddy, it's not my fault," says Walt, "so here's all you can do. Take that piece of tarp back there and build yourself a lean-to. You can have the blankets and flashlights too, and when I get back I'll get another truck off to you."

"Not on your jesus life. Give us a blanket."

Someone handed Will a blanket, which he wrapped around his top half, leaving only his eyes showing, and after he tucked that one into his belt, he grabbed another one, overlapped the first one and covered his bottom half. All of this he bound to his body with a long piece of rope. The end of which he gave someone to secure on the inside. He then planted his feet firmly on the running board, gripped an outside frame, faced the back end, and uttered a muffled, "Let's go."

"You're out of your head. That's a good sixty miles we got to do, an' look at this weather," said Walt. "You're stayin' here. I ain't goin' to be responsible."

"Shut yer gob an' get goin'! I'm freezin' out here." And that's the way they started back.

Well, of course, you know that there's no way it's going to come off smooth. It was agreed upon that Will would hammer on the side of the roof if he was in trouble, but once he got into a semicomfortable position, he sailed her through, because he got so numb, and his blankets stiffened up so that he couldn't afford the shift in position or even take the chance of letting go long enough to knock, relying then, only on one hand.

But even at that, he might have been all right if they hadn't come to a particular turn at Rattling Brook and a whole new storm, which made off with Will's bottom blanket, taking it over the tree tops like one of them flying carpets and making the world of difference in his body temperature.

Now, Will had a thing about underwear. He never wore any. Well, I won't say never. If Mary, his sister, could ever slow him down long enough to get him into a pair, he'd manage to put up with them. But there's nothing wrong with that. "Neider did Marilyn Monroe wear 'em," said Will. "She said, it interfered wit the line of 'er body. Same wit me. So she give 'em up altogedder. Proper ting, too!"

Now, I suppose you're going to say, "But surely to god he'd wear long johns out on a search in the winter." And you'd be right. He had them, all right, but see, eight of the fifteen buttons were gone, and guess what eight.

Well, how do I tell the rest of it, without it sounding too coarse, which I don't mean it to be. Anyway, it's the truth, for God's sake, so what odds?

There he was with his eight buttons—gone. And since the whole body was so paralyzed by now, a fella would hardly notice if—well, let's say this. Let's say—

You take a man without a thumb who cuts the thumb out of his mitt, not having any need for it, then gives the mitt to someone who's got a thumb. That was how it was. Just like that; so that's the way Will came back that night, and that's why Will Cole went to St. John's, the first time, three years ago.

But for all that, there didn't seem to be any telltale signs of that old ailment on the eve of the more recent St. John's trip, as he leaned out the bottom window of the big, old, square, red, plain "boarding" house—well, no it wasn't a boarding house really—more like a "transient" house. Well, let me say this, the girls who rested there had jobs around the town and had, at one time or another, come from elsewhere. Anyway, Will thought them a grand lot and found great pleasure in whiling away an hour or two of a dull afternoon in a harmless game or two of "strip checkers" (a game of his own invention), and other such delights.

He had his moth-eaten old overnight bag in there with him and planned on walking straight over to the railway station when his "shopping" was done.

"Come on in," he shouted, "Carol won't mind." The Carol he referred to I had known for a long time now, and *that* Carol *would* mind, I told him, especially since the wedding was coming up.

"You want me to pick up something? That'd be nice, wouldn't it?"

"No, but Marian is in here, askin' for ya."

"Which one is she? Oh, the big one with the bad legs?"

According to Will, she looked good, and had taken off twenty pounds.

"Well, taking off weight ain't likely to fix her eyes," I said.

This set him off in a roar of laughter. "Hear that, Marian?" Will shouted back over his shoulder.

"Who wants him?" was the answer, and I was forced to back off from the window sill as she rushed by Will's shoulder and half out the window with a broken-off broom. But she didn't get me.

"Andrew, my son," she said, "It's time the good little boys were home in bed, isn't it?"

I made a face at her. "Oh, careful now or I'll come out there, and you know what happened last time." Then she went back in.

"They got a Dutch girl in here now. Just off the boat. Wooden shoes an' all. Come on, Dutch, for God's sake."

"No. I'll see you at work in the morning." I said.

"I won't be there. I'm off to St. John's—soon's I'm through in here."

"Again? I'd like to know what you've got hidden out there. I've told you to let me know when you were going next, so I can get time off too."

He told me I couldn't afford the energy, and to save it for Carol. I would've torn his head off, but I misjudged it and he got the window down on my shirt sleeve and laughed his ass off at me through the glass, until I pulled it loose and lost a button.

It worked out in his favour again. The ignorant thing, I thought, as I made my way across the parking lot towards my brother Cec's truck.

I only had a few yards to go when Ruth Lowe's Volks swung onto the lot and arrived right in front of me. Holy dyin'! It was either very funny, or not funny at all.

"Hello Andrew, how've you been?"

And I said, "Fine Ruth. How've you been?" (while Will was carrying on inside the big red house just a parking lot away and probably half undressed by now).

Somewhere around here, I discovered I had X-ray vision because I swear that during that little talk with that sweet Ruth, I could see everything that was going on inside there. I don't know why I was so bloody worried. He'd have no reason to show his head and she'd have no reason to know he had his checker board out.

"Where you going?" I asked.

"Botwood. To see some friends."

"Oh, yes, that's wonderful." (What the hell was wonderful about that?)

"Have you seen Will lately?" she asked.

I looked toward the front windows of the house. "Oh yes."

"How is he?"

"He's in good shape."

"Busy, I suppose, is he?"

"That's for sure."

Will, dressed only in a shirt, was chasing a very long,

thin girl around the room. I started to sweat for some reason, and I'm positive I couldn't have sounded too natural.

"He never slows down, does he?" she asked.

"No."

"You've been with him and talked to him. Do you see any change coming?"

"No."

She was determined not to get mad. "I get the feeling he wants people to think he's wilder than he really is "

Oh, I don't know, I thought, as Will's bare bottom flew over a bedstead and onto his screeching victim below. (Perhaps big Marian with the broad back and white socks, or the hollow-eyed little Vera who was always afraid of being kicked out because of Will's hooting and hollering.)

"But isn't it funny," said Ruth, "he's still likeable."

A girl with wild, ropey black hair was vaccinating Will's neck with an enormous, permanent hickey.

"Generous too," I added.

Here Will (he told me later) checked his wallet. "All right. Who the Christ has my ten dollars? I had seven tens and there's one gone."

"He never seems to care about what other people say about him," said Ruth.

"Why should he? People have been trying to make him look bad for a long time."

"Are you talking about me, Andrew?"

"I never said *you*." I looked at my feet.

"You looked straight at me," she said.

Will was roaring around by now, pulling out drawers, looking under mattresses. "If I don't get dat ten dollars, I'll string the lot of ya up by your—"

A sort of half-Chinese girl was trying to look innocent. "You got it, ya slant-eyed whore," yelled Will. "Gimme me ten bucks, you maggoty mainlander," and the two of them went up and down the walls.

"Come on now Andrew," said Ruth, "you keep hanging around Will because you like to have a crippled duck around you. Tell the truth."

72

I got loud. "Who's talking about *ducks* for Jesus' sake? If I could lose that ignorant thing tomorrow, I'd be all set."

I must have suddenly lost my X-ray gift, because all I could see inside was a great colourful flurry of inhuman shapes and objects.

I asked Ruth if she had made up her mind about going to Toronto.

"Not really. I can't make myself move. I think I'm happy enough. I should be in a hurry, but I'm not. I don't feel the time going by but, unlike Will, I know it is. I feel exactly the same way every morning when I wake up because I suppose I feel exactly the same each night before—Oh my, all of this sounds *awful.*"

She touched my arm, and I wondered where she was getting her loving.

"Andrew, I didn't mean what I said about the crippled duck thing. You know that, don't you?"

It didn't matter to me, because I didn't know what it meant.

She switched her mood, perhaps never to talk about those things again.

"I miss our school days—they were simple—I don't know—"

Thank God she was lost in her school-day thoughts and didn't see the back door of the big red house come flying open and the Chinese girl and our mutual friend come roaring out. She, trying to tie the string on her skimpy silk robe; and the other one, all arms and legs. She had a good lead until Will got his pants zipped up, and then he was off, leaping over any unexpected obstacle and taking the corners of the house at a good thirty.

All that Ruth might have heard was the loudmouth, Marian, who shouted, "Go Betty, go," from an open window and Will's, "Shut yer mout'," in passing—but she must have figured they were kid's sounds.

I was almost too intrigued with the race to hear Ruth start up her Volks.

"Goodbye Andrew."

"Goodbye Ruth," I said, and I stepped aside, as her little car bounced up onto the gravel road and got on its way, leaving one with a sense of guilt and wonderment for the girl who still worked in the Royal Bank, who still, at approximately our age, lived with her folks, and who seemed to have gotten herself lost somehow. Like her little Volks which now finds itself in the middle of a parade of impatient, larger cars, she's travelling at the wrong speed, perhaps. Plus the fact she has her mind on the wrong people, if Will Cole happens to be one of them; and judging from his behaviour with the well-dressed, forty-eight-year-old lady on the train to St. John's, she'd be better off with her glass of warm milk and a book.

*　　*　　*　　*　　*

The lady had been reading, but had taken off her glasses and nestled in the corner of her seat, after a quick glance outside at the darkening sky.

Her eyes opened, closed again, reopened and caught Will grinning at her from his seat across the way. How would you like to open your eyes and find that ignorant thing staring at you, and chewing on a great big Macintosh apple?

He offered her a bite. She closed her eyes. When she opened them again, he'd split the apple down the middle and offered her half. She looked disgusted. Next he reached in his paper bag, brought out an orange, and looked at her.

She shook her head, almost violently, and turned to face the window—but when he buried his face in the open bag, came up with a banana and decided not to offer it, she smiled slightly against her will and tried to get back into her book.

She probably wouldn't be interested in a game of checkers, but he pulled the broken and bent old board out of his back pocket, his plastic bag full of checkers out of that beat-up old overnight case, and waited for the woman to accept. She didn't.

OK, figured Will, I'll just sit here and charm da pants off her, and I'll be goddamned if that didn't do it.

For the next few minutes, he got her into a staring match. His expression didn't alter in the slightest. The plan was to just sit there, arms folded, and twinkle her right on her back. That's if the conductor would get his duties over with and he could find a blanket from somewhere.

But first things first. She wasn't going to be bullied into it. She'd do a little knitting. That might take her mind off this slightly coarse but oddly erotic individual, who, when not looking her in the eye and making her show signs of wanting to smile, was looking at her jiggling front—and when she covered that considerable expanse with her knitting, would go exploring further south. But mainly it was her eyes he was interested in. If you can't win over the head, you'll never win the rest.

She's squirming, thought Will. And before you could ask what he would do next, he was holding her wool, while she wound up a new ball, and their knees were bumping. Which is pretty good for a start.

By the time the wool had run out, they knew that they'd have to have their minds made up, and when the last loop had fallen off Will's hands, she was nodding and breathing and smiling and twitching something fierce.

A quick and furtive trip up the aisle (in stocking feet) got Will, not a blanket, but a raincoat from a sleeping old man who wouldn't have come around for a cannon's roar.

In a matter of a minute, they were wrapped in the raincoat, wrapped in her wool, and wrapped in themselves. And by the time the other passengers were ready to wake up, and the conductor showed his face at the far end of the coach, there were sounds coming up from underneath that poor man's raincoat like the breathing of two asthmatic mountain goats.

"ST. JOHN'S. St. John's next," the conductor shouted and swayed his way up the aisle, stopping to rouse a screech-filled lumberjack (who had spent the trip down between the seats), picking up newspapers and rolling Coke bottles; doffing his cap, smiling, and assisting our lady with her knitting (or what was left of it) before he went out the

75

door to the next car, where he passed Will coming back from taking a breath of fresh air.

"Morning, skipper," said Will, starting for the door that the conductor held open for him.

"Didn't take us that long in the old days," the man said, as Will passed by. Then they both laughed and laughed and laughed together until the train came into the station, where the last one to get off was a sleepy old man who couldn't figure out what he did with his raincoat. But he found it, anyway, just a few seats up the aisle.

Meanwhile the woman was grabbing Will's arm for balance as she got down onto the platform. "I promised I'd have that sweater finished," she said, finding the memory of the whole thing very funny, and although she was having a bit of trouble pulling herself into shape, Will thought she looked even better than she had the previous night—with a fresh new glow on her un-made-up face and a spring in her step. And he told her so.

"Are you sure that's a compliment?" she asked. "Now look, you're staying how long?"

"Oh, about a week. Somewhere in dere."

"And you mean you won't have time to give me a call? Listen—Oh, you're lovely you are—Here!" She came out of her purse with a pen. "Just a second, don't run off yet—I need some paper." Her hair was falling in her eyes again, but she didn't bother to get rid of it. "Here! This is where you can get me—I'll put it on the back of one of my husband's business cards. You promise now?"

Will told her that the afternoons and evenings weren't too good, but if she didn't mind the mornings, he could work it.

"I don't care if it's ten minutes a day in a store window. You call," she said, " 'cause you're lovely, you are."

"Tanks," said Will, and he was off up the platform.

Suddenly, after what seemed like ages, "WILL!" It was the woman again. Will stopped and cocked a hand over his ear to get the message. "Don't forget," she screamed, and Will waved, turned, jiggled his head in disbelief, and turned his fresh new grin into a roar of raucous laughter as he stepped off the platform and swaggered into the sunshiny Saturday of Water Street in the city of St. John's.

After he'd bounced out of the liquor store and shoved his bottle of screech into his shapeless old bag, he whipped into the very next store, emerged with a package, and stopped to take in a couple of mannequins (one dressed and one undressed) in the window of that very store.

He was only allowed to look at them for a second, before the man stepped into the window from inside and put a pair of pants on her. Next came the brassiere.

He noticed Will's sly face between the skirt and the blouse, but managed to get it all on. As he started to undress the dressed one, he mouthed a "PISS OFF" to Will, and got rid of her silver suit.

Next came the brassiere. One strap at a time. By now the man had just about refused to continue, with this monkey grinning up at him and making him feel like a dirty old man. Doing things with his eyes was bad enough, but panting, and slurping and making sounds like a dog were making the man sick.

Then came the pants. Fast! And wasn't Will there for that one, sir! Then he checked his watch and hurried away. Stopped. Kept an old lady company crossing the street. Kept another old lady company coming back again, and decided he really had to get going; and from what he told me about the way it started out on the train, he did get going, and no mistake about it.

SHIRLEY McCORMACK, R.N.

"Stan is me first name. Stan is me last name. Me name is Stan. And don't tink I'm sick, because I'm not, and don't tink I'm goin' to die, because I'm not. I just come in 'ere because dey kicked me off da streets, an' I dropped me uppers off da wharf." But later on he told me, "A fella needs someone to 'ave a small talk wit' now an' agin, an' a small room to 'is ownself wit' a clean pot to put 'is h'arse down into and wit' people who idden all da time kickin' 'im because he smells bad. Does ya tink I smells bad?"

"Yes. Something awful," I said.

"Well, you can go ta 'ell too," he said.

I was his nurse for his last three and a half years. I'm twenty-seven years of age. Red hair and blue eyes. I'm a bit on the fat side and not as pretty as anyone.

I'd had a bloody great fight with my boy friend the night before so I wasn't in too good a mood the day that old Stan came in here; but maybe it was because of that dirty mood that we got off on the right foot.

We've done a lot of cursing and swearing at each other in three and one-half years. He kept threatening to report me for the language and the tricks I'd play on him when he was bad, but he knew that he mightn't get someone else who suited him as well.

We also knew, the both of us, that when he'd hit his low spots and it came to the matter of dying, I couldn't pull him back.

There was only one person who could do that for him, Will, a man from Grand Falls. And whenever Stan knew he was coming to see him, he'd have one great big scrap with me and fire me. Like a child who dismisses the friend who'd been playing with him all day because a new friend had come along.

"What da cursed hell's flame is da matter wit' ya? Can't you do anyting right?" he says. "Jumpin' Jesus, yer some

79

stunned. Get out! Get yer h'ugly face away from me. Dis is my room. Bugger off!"

On these occasions, about three weeks apart, I'd let him shout on, because I knew that not only were my services not required but not really effective.

So I'd leave him alone to wait for his friend. He knew that Will would arrive on the same day each time, so his fight with me would start up about three hours before. Although there was a time when he came a day late. Stan got fidgety as hell and wanted to call me back, but instead he got himself another nurse to make me jealous. She annoyed him all to hell, and when she came to me with the story of how he ran his knobby old hand up her uniform when she was changing his sheets and she threatened to really make it tough on him, I said (I never took to Alice Penn atall), "That's too bad my dear," I said, "I should've told him he'd never find anything up there."

On Saturdays he'd be a different man. We'd wash his snow-white hair, get him into the cherry-red sweater that I got off old Mr. Cowley who died down the hall, slap his colourful toque on his head, and we'd go for a stomp out the back—and could he stomp when he finally got going! He'd roll up his great fists, set his chin, lift his knees and literally stomp, stomp, stomp out the back door around the lot and back again to his waiting chair. He couldn't do it for long, but long enough for you to see a trace of the type of man he must have been.

He was his best on Saturdays because he was a Saturday night man, you could tell. He was a man who set out to be a legend, and from what I hear he came pretty close. And now, when his ravings toward me had come and gone, the strong dignity in the man would come out, and I'd almost want to sit at his knee and have him comfort me like a father.

And his voice. You'd swear you'd been with him all his life long. Tasting his very food and his drink. You could hear the dry twigs crackling under his logans as he walked the country, and feel flushed in the face by his night fires.

He was the father I never had and the adventurer I wanted to be.

He had a kindness for the Island. And *only* for his Newfoundland—but before I begin to sound too dull, let *him* tell you what else he was.

"Nuttin'! Not a jeezly ting could I put me hand to and make a livin' out of 'er, but dat didn't bodder me, maid. What I did, I did da best I could. I could certainly drink down da rum an' I never 'eard any complaints from da girls. Now an' agin, I'd be told to leave some outport or odder because dey didn't like da way I was carryin' on; but—I was never one to hang aroun' one place too long. Yes, I been in jail once or twice—once, dey said, I come into dis little small place an' it was Sunday an' no stores open, an' I 'ad to stock up. So I killed a cow, dey said, an' was on me way up da coast wit' me sackful of steaks an' chops when dey got me. Dat's what dey tells me anyway. Da odder time was when dey said I made sport wit dis ranger by tying 'im to a big spruce tree, peein' on 'im, an' den leavin' 'im. Dat was nuttin' but da biggest kind of lie. It wasn't a spruce atall. It was most prob'ly a fir, an' fer da odder part—dat's filty, dat is, an' ya just look at me an' tell me if I looks like da kind of fella who would do a filty ting like dat, now."

I looked at him and nodded vigorously.

"Den yer nuttin' but dirt yerself so git out."

I told Will Cole the truth. How I really felt. That the periods of depression and weakness were getting longer and longer.

But I never really got to know Will Cole. He seemed nice enough, but not one a girl could turn her front to. I know one thing, any time he'd come through the front door to the home, he looked as though he were on a great secret mission. And I suppose in a way, he certainly was. To keep old Stan going.

There seemed to be a reason behind it all, beyond him just caring for Stan—almost as though there were only two like them in the world, and to lose one would be a most terrible tragic thing. The extent of which would be known only to Will.

Will was holding a package and listening hard to my every word. "There's no pain you know. I told him you'd be coming to see him, because this time he'd forgotten when it was, exactly. He seemed happy, because he blasted me a bit, but then he began to fade—a bit each hour. Every time I'd peek in his room I'd expect the worst. He's not good, as he is now."

Will uncreased his brow and headed for the open balcony door. There he found Stan, all alone on the big balcony, white, bent, and lost-looking. Will walked right into Stan's line of vision and was surprised that he didn't react. He walked towards him a few steps and stopped. Still nothing. He continued this until he was practically on top of Stan, then unwrapped his gift, a bright red shirt, held it out in front of him, and broke into his beautiful grin. "All right. Put dis on now an' we'll take a day off."

Nothing.

"Skipper? Ya comin' wit me? Stan! It's me!"

"Dat you Will?"

"Sure it's me."

"How're ya gettin' on Will?"

"Number one. How about you?"

Stan slips back to his former thoughtful self. He turns his head away. Will steps in front of him again—not letting up on his attack.

"Don't tell me yer not glad to see me, an' me comin' all dis way," said Will.

"I'm some tired Will."

"Yer tired? Jesus, how would ya like to have been sluggin' away in da bloody paper mill all week?"

"Oh, yer young for God's sake."

Will told him they were the same age, and that the only difference was that Will did more "strappin' and drinkin'" than Stan. "And dat's what keeps me in shape." (He was sounding more and more like the old reprobate in the wheelchair.)

"Never mind," said Will, "You an' me is goin' to have a walk in a while. Get da old juices goin'—have a few jugs— slap a little nugget in da hair; an' come dis evenin', I'll smuggle a couple of live ones into yer room. By tomorrow morning, da only ting dat'll be wrong wit' you will be a touch of da old stingers. All right?"

Stan was chuckling and wheezing like an old flame come back to life. He wiped a string of spittle off his chin with the sleeve of poor old Mr. Cowley's red sweater. "All right Will. If you want me to."

These trips—down the main walk, and up and down Water Street—were, without fail, uneventful and a bloody great bore to the old man. And he certainly showed Will that he felt it, for from one end of the outing to his return, he did nothing but criticize. The clothes in the shop windows: "Look at da cost of dat rag dere, an' it barely coverin' 'er h'arse."

The policeman: "Look at dat sweet young ting. A baby for Lord's sake. Let me give 'im a good kick."

The city: "Is dis Water Street? Dis idden Water Street. I knows Water Street."

Even Will: "Yer walkin' too fast. Hang 'er down 'ere, else I'm goin' ta smack ya in da face."

And so on.

Will let it all roll off. He had the old duffer on his feet, that was good enough for him. The two of them—making their way, stopping, starting, sitting, standing, and Stan, complaining and whining and having a rotten old time—began to resemble one another in a way. They could even have been father and son. Same type. Same way of life, and over the three and a half year period, they would use each other's expressions and finally they were laughing and walking alike (when you could get Stan to forget his ailments).

One thing for sure, and I'm more certain of it now than I've ever been, they were two of a kind. The only pair like it in the store.

Will would deliver Stan back to his room and, settled in his chair, the old guy would have a whole new string of complaints and criticisms:

"Ya said ya was goin' to take me up to da Crow's Nest for a drink of rum an' ya didn't do it, so ya didn't."

"That's fifty-nine steps up," said Will. "Ya'd never have done it."

"Dat's a lie. Ya just didn't want to take me up dere. You was in too big a rush ta—ta—ta get me back in 'ere. I shouldn't 'ave let ya put me in 'ere anyway. I don't like it atall. I should 'ave a 'ouse of me own."

"I didn't put ya in here. *You* put ya in here."

"I did not."

"Ya did."

"Liar, liar, big, big liar."

"Ya came in here over three years ago when ya had no place else to go."

"Who da bloody 'ell told you dat? I 'ad tons of places to go, my sonny b'ys. Tons."

"Give us da name of one."

"An'—an'—an' ya said we was goin' to find girls too an' we didn't, so we didn't."

"Now, what would you do wit a girl? What?"

The old man's juices were really going now, and Will was thrilled with his temporary recovery.

"Oh—oh—I'd—ya know what I'd do . . . you know. I'd— I'd—Oh-h-o-o-o-o-w-e-e. I'd KISS 'em! I'd KISS 'em!"

"Dat it, den?" said Will, "Sure, dat's nuttin'."

"Well—I'd tickle 'em under da arms."

"Jesus. Dey'd love dat."

"And den—watch out! Watch out! I'd get all foolish wit 'em—an' get all—you knows. Hee-hee—you bugger—you knows. Ya just wants me to say it, an' I don't have to if I don't want to."

"Good enough. Now we'll have a small game of checkers."

"Not now Will."

Stan stopped twinkling suddenly and was lost a bit, as before. Will thought he'd read something to him.

"Later Will. Can I talk to ya 'bout someting?"

"Sure."

Stan was afraid Will would get mad with him so he changed his mind. Will kept at him, and Stan changed the subject. Laughing again.

"I 'members when I first saw ya," said Stan. "Tree years

ago, wasn't it? ya were comin' along da road out dere. Drunk ya were. An' I was sittin' under da big tree by da gate."

"An' look at ya, still. The heart goin' like a jackhammer."

Stan turned serious again. "Will, I haven't got any money."

"Dat's not news."

"The only ting I do have—is here." He reached to his dresser and came out with a tin box. I'd seen it from time to time but we hadn't really discussed it.

It was old enough, that's for sure, and on the lid were the oval, coloured likenesses of King George V and Queen Mary, framed in gold leaf. I remembered the kind of box immediately because my mother used to keep tea in one just like it.

He showed Will a few letters and a couple of snaps that could have been pictures of anyone really, they were that faded and cracked. A First World War medal, awarded him for some reason he couldn't remember. (As it turned out it was simply an overseas medal.) He offered it to Will who turned it down. Then came his discharge papers. Will was suddenly interested in these, and taking them from the old man, he opened them carefully because of their condition and went searching for Stan's last name, which Will had never known.

It was gone. It had been right on the crease and it had now been completely obliterated. His first name had almost suffered the same fate, but thank God it was saved, else, we would've had to invent one for him.

"What's your last name Stan?"

"What?"

"What's yer last name?"

"Stan's good enough."

"Can I see yer letters?" asked Will.

"Dese letters?" said Stan, holding them like he might have their sender. "Dese are from Florence Healey."

Her name came as easily and swiftly to his tongue as any word might, and you just *knew* he was talking about something very special and dear.

"That's the one I should've held onto." There were tears in his eyes, suddenly.

"Go on," said Will. "Ya were like I am. Ya had too much goin' on, ta settle down."

"Oh—I was awful in dose days, all right."

"Ya don't have to tell me 'bout ya, my son. I heard all of dat when I was a child. Dem stories was all over da Island. My old man used to say ya should've been hung for the tings ya did."

"What was 'is name again?" asked Stan.

"Arthur Cole," Will said.

Stan shifted in his chair and puffed out his chest in a most superior way. "Never 'eard of 'im," he said, having asked the same question fifty times.

Will shook his head and grinned as Stan raised his fingertips to his lips and furrowed his brow in deep remembering.

"I made da rounds of dis island a hundred times or more —leaving 'em on the trail, one by one, an' not so much as a final look behind to remember deir faces—"

He then looked at the letters. "But 'ere, now—dis one could 'ave given me da kind of life I never 'ad. Dey're sweet letters, Will. You'll take 'em for me, won't ya?"

Will took them, partly expecting to find the old man's full name on an envelope, but there were no envelopes. He opened them, read a "Dear Stanley" and gave them back.

"Will, don't be foolish. It won't be long for me."

"Here now—" said Will, wanting to throw him off the subject, but not being too successful. "Here. Get in yer chair."

"No." said Stan. "I won't."

"Get in! We're goin' out on da balcony."

Stan got in and Will wheeled him down the corridor and out the door to the balcony and the fresh air. Too fresh really, because Stan had trouble keeping his toque on his head.

"My Lord," said Will, taking in St. John's. "Every time I come out here I see a whole new string of buildings. What's goin' up over dere d'ya s'pose?"

"I just started tinkin 'bout da letters, that's all. What

happens to da letters?" He couldn't be stopped. "I got no one. Do dey burn 'em, I wonder? Or t'row 'em away? Da letters don't die. Da love in 'em an' all. Den where do dey go? You take 'em for me, Will, so's I'll know where dey are."

"Shut up Stan! Shut up about dyin'. That's enough!"

Stan seemed as strong as he ever was, almost as if Will had planned the whole thing.

"*You* shut up," said Stan. "*I* can say whatever I want in here. Take da box an' go. I'm tired of lookin' at ya."

"Want me to go, do ya?"

"Yes, I do, yes."

Will was nudging Stan's arm and annoying the hell out of him. "Sure? Want me to go?"

"Yes, yes. Go now, go."

Will, with the box, stepped off towards the door. "All right. If you want me to go, I'll go." Then, he very quietly snuck up behind Stan and dropped the tin box in his lap. "But I'm not takin' the box. Long as it's here, you'll be here. I'll see ya tomorrow."

Then, with a wild, crazy laugh, Will jumps up and down in the air, makes a foolish face at Stan, who has struggled out of the chair, swearing, then takes off through the balcony door.

"Ya stubborn young bastard. Take my letters. Come on now! Come on Will! Take da bloody box."

Will was passing Reverend Davis who was on his way into old Mrs. Hall's room when Stan finally appeared in the balcony doorway, and shouted:

"Ya son of a bitch," straight at the Reverend's face, and left him standing there in ignorant amazement.

It's none of my business what Will Cole did between the time he left the hospital and returned the following day, but whoever he did it with sure didn't leave much for another day. The only thing left was his grin, and how he still had strength left over for that, I'll never know. But what an apparition came up the walk, through the door and, with boots in hand and soaking stocking-feet, dragging down the long corridor towards the desk. Now *how* did he get so wet?

His answer was that he was short on time and had to do *it* in the poor woman's shower with his clothes on. I told him that was an old joke, and he said "Who do ya tink told it da first time?"

So either he was lying and the story that Alice Penn told about seeing someone sitting under our fountain down by the gate was true—or I was in at the start of another legend.

"What da hell sense is dere in cartin' da chair up 'ere," said Stan, standing on the big hill directly in back of the home.

"You were the one who wanted it when we started out," Will said, and collapsed in the chair himself.

"Dat's mine, get out of it."

"Are you goin' to use it?"

"Maybe I will."

Will gave up the chair and sat on a rock.

Stan was in his critical mood again. "I didn't want to come outside today."

Will didn't answer.

"I didn't get a jeezly wink of sleep last night, eider."

Nothing from Will except a word or two of "I'se the b'y."

"I didn't want to come outside," he said again.

By now Will is tapping his feet and the song is getting louder until, like magic, he's got the old fellow humming along, as if he didn't have a complaint in his head.

> I'se da b'y who builds da boat
> An' I'se da b'y who sails 'er
> I'se da b'y who catches da fish
> An' brings 'em home to Lizer—

Will has picked up a couple of sticks and is putting them to work on the boulder in front of him, in time to the song. This brings old Stan to life and on a pair of feet, unlike his usual ones, he performs to the "chin" music, vocal though it is, and while the dust is still in the air, he flops down on a rock and laughs the laugh of a happy child.

Will, attempting to continue the mood, grabs the wheelchair and takes off over the rocks, through the bushes, down old and new trails, working the chair like a toy, bouncing it off rocks, till he has it in the air, swings it around and around, and he's off again, with a TAHDIDDERAH, TAHDIDDERAH, TAHDIDDERAH! and arrives back at Stan's rock, where the old man has been helpless with laughter at his foolish friend's antics.

"Come on old man. Hop in! Yer next," said Will, breathlessly. Stan, laughing too hard to speak, just shakes his head.

This being the case, Will whips Stan's tin box out of his lap and puts it on the canvas chair seat. "All right," says Will. "We'll give old Florence Healey a ride. Come on, Flo my darlin'." And he's off, before Stan has a chance to interfere. After only a weave and a twist, a wheel stopped short at a rock, the box went flying, and out came the letters—going in every direction, but mainly down the slope.

Will stopped long enough to shoot a fast sick smile up to the angry Stan on the ridge.

"Get 'em ya dumb bastard," screamed the purple old man, then sat on the ridge while Will scrambled around for the letters, which weren't all that easy to find. In fact, he came back one letter short and Stan was quick to mention it. Will returned to the bottom of the slope, and found it and returned it, although Stan had already decided never to speak to Will again and maybe give him a kick or two in the leg. Neither one of his kicks connected, which added to his fury.

"Yer a bugger, ya know dat Will? Ya gets me so excited."

"It's good for ya." Will opened the first of a half-dozen beers brought along for the occasion. "Want one?"

Stan was still in high volume. "You knows bloody well dat I don't drink beer. I drinks RUM, an' you never brings any wit ya."

The truth was he couldn't take either. There were lots of reasons, but one was that it ran right through him just when he'd have his mind on something else.

"All the excitement is over, an' ya won't have to come out all this way to see me anymore."

"Ya don't want me to come out anymore?"

" 'ave ya gone deaf? Dat's what I just said. 'Cause I won't be 'ere—dat's what I meant."

It was Will's turn to rant. "Y'see? Dere ya go. You're not in any pain now are ya?"

"No. Don't 'ave a pain in me body—I'm just exhausted. There's not a hell of a lot of air left in da tire, Will."

Will grabbed Stan suddenly and turned him in the direction of a couple of young picknickers, making their way up the slope and heading their way.

"Hey. Look at dat! What d'ya tink of dat, old man? Now, where d'ya s'pose dey're goin'?"

"Wha'?—wha'?—who?—wha'?"

"Right dere look. Don't let 'em see us. Come on, get down here."

He managed to get the old man off the rock and crouched behind the boulder. "See. I'll bet dey're goin' ta head straight for da woods. You just wait an' see if dey don't."

Stan is protesting.

"Den after dey gets settled, an' he's all set to go, you and me are goin' to walk on t'rough dere. Just walkin'. Casual as hell, an' pretendin' not to notice, see? But we'll stop right where dey are, see? I know. I'll stop to light a smoke—an'—an'—"

"Will!" shouts Stan.

"What?"

"WILL!" he shouts louder. "I'm fed up."

"Goddammit, Stan, yer lettin' go. There's lots of time. We should have brought me checkers, ta get yer mind off it."

Stan watches him, as if for the very first time.

"What're ya lookin' at me like dat for?"

Stan does indeed sound as though he hasn't much air left.

"Why d'ya always go on like dat—all the time? Why can't I have a little rest, like odder old people? I could be happy enough Will—just sittin' and waitin' for it. I likes ya to come an' see me, but Jesus, I never heard of such carry-on. See, I'm old an' I knows it an' I lives wit' it. I lives my way an' I'm goin' to die my way. Now dere's nuttin' wrong wit dat is dere? Why can't ya just come an visit—'ave a cup of tea wit' me an' go again till the next time? Dat'd be fine wit' me. Dere's no need of ya burstin' into my room an' telling me 'bout all da young girls you been wit an' takin' me down on dat street to show me da shop windows. Dose tings in the windows are for young people an dat's not me, so why d'ya go on about it?"

Will became Stan's strength again and had to have it his way, if his plan to keep Stan alive was ever to work. It might have been Stan speaking as a young man: "Cause you an' me are da good times. Ya did da Island a hundred times over. You'd see da rocks, an' coves an' fill up on da spring water in da woods, an' even now, ya remember the smells of tings." Then when he thinks he's going to lose him again, he lays it on. "An' da women? Dose two sisters over in Come-by-Chance when ya had yer boat—an' da rum runnin'—wasn't dat da way to live?"

The old man is almost there. Will goes on.

"You can't give dat up, old man. It'd be a sin. Yer da same man *now!*"

Stan is nodding and making funny little baby sounds.

". . . an' it's not da first time I filled up me old tin lizzy an' took 'er down into da bay, to look for girls—"

At the moment, Will doesn't much care that it's bordering delirium. He's got him smiling and relaxed.

"What muscles, dey said. What muscles ya got. I love ya, dey'd say. Hang on here for a spell, won't ya?"

He raises his knotty hand, pushes his toque off his head and weaves his fingers in and around his thinning snow white hair.

"Tell me where ya got yer black, curly hair. They went for da hair."

He stops. Will prods him to get him going again, like you might an old gramophone. "An' what else, Stan?" Will says.

"If she'd 'ave held onto da reins a bit looser, she wouldn't have fell outa the cart. Almost spiled da picnic. But it was nice all da same. We had a couple of big lobster wit us, an' den'—" here he got sly and made Will wait for the juiciest part. "Afterwards—under da tree—some good, my son. Ya know, she hardly complained about her broken foot—so I took her home to a doctor—as fast as I could—"

Then he was amazingly normal. "Ya stayin' for supper, Will?"

"I don't know, what're dey havin?" said Will, much happier now that he had Stan back.

Their next few hours were to be their last together, but they were happy hours. Stan talked and talked and talked about his future plans. A nice soft job with lots of pay and a new hat and shoes. Maybe he'd do a turn in the lumberwoods again. Just till he got a pocketful of money. He pounded his wheelchair with each and every remembrance.

And Will would add to them, keeping him supplied with fresh vigour and colour, until they'd begin to sound like a couple of children, planning what they would do when school was out. Will talked about Stan's friends in St. Pierre. That'd be great. Drop a little rum off down there "an' tear da bloody lid right off."

Will hadn't seen half the places that Stan had, so Stan would be his calling card as they went in and out of the bays looking for women.

"Lovely, tell your mother!" Will would shout, and drown his face in beer. "Give us sometin' in French now. If we're goin' to St. Pierre, I want to know all da good words. I never had a touch of da *parlez-vous*. Ya have though, haven't ya, ya old snake? Come on now—how do ya say—'Hello, me dear, dat's a fine lookin' ting you got dere.' No —no—give us, 'It's a grand day,'—or anyting atall. Hey Stan, how old d'ya s'pose dem two sisters would be by now?"

*   *   *   *   *

We only lost one of our old people in the fire. If Will hadn't passed out from his night at the El Tico, he might have heard the sirens. He might even have seen the flickering flames on the wall of the bedroom.

My boy friend arrived to find me shouting at a fireman. Hysterical is what I was, I suppose, but he held his own and told me to go to hell. That they had done all that could be done.

"If they're not out now, they're not comin' out," he shouted. I can't help it. We tried, goddammit! Now keep out of the way."

"But I can't find Stan." I was screaming by now and my boy friend was holding me and wiping my dirty face.

Then I saw another fireman coming out from the back, holding Stan's tin box. He told me the man was on his way out when he broke away from the fireman and went back through the smoke. "Lord God. You should have seen him, fighting me off when I tried to hold onto him. Jesus, he was strong. I tried to find a couple of different openings but I couldn't. I kept on yelling to him but he wouldn't have cared anyway, the way he was acting. Then I was going to try knocking down a wall to see if there was another way, when I'll be goddamned if I didn't see him, almost towering above the smoke and holding this tin box over his head. 'The box. The box' he kept saying. 'Give Will the box.' I'd never have reached it in a hundred years, and the smoke and fire came right up over him. Do you know what happened? Just when I figured he was gone, the box came whistling out through the flames, and bounced off the wall beside me. It was a hard throw. You'd almost say he was mad at me, the way that thing came out of there. Then I thought. Why didn't he try it himself? He might've made it, y'know?"

I cried. Oh, how I cried. The fireman left us and headed for the coffee, when he met Will roaring down off the main road and told him what I'm glad I didn't have to tell him. "There was one old feller—he was all—"

After that, Will walked over to me, without taking his eyes off the almost-dead fire. "Sure it was him," said Will, with little effort and a certain degree of bitterness which surprised me. "Has to be, doesn't it? He *would've* been da only one, an' he *could've* done it, but he laid down. Dat's Stan all right."

I almost wanted to smack him across the face for being so callous about it, and I don't know why I didn't, except for the fact that I didn't know him that well, and there must have been some deep reason for saying it the way he did.

Then I handed him the box. He looked at it in my hands for the longest time. I asked if he would be around for a few days.

"What for?" he said, "He's dead now."

And as he took the box from me and started up the slope towards the road, he could've been crying.

I hoped he was.

ANDREW SCOTT

Aside from the story about the woman on the train, he had just one tale to tell me when he got back. Which made him about three stories shy of his usual record for a weekly visit.

Will, by the way, is the perfectionist that one takes him for by the way he tells a story. He's honest enough to describe it the way he sees it, and there have been times that his descriptions of certain female companions would throw a normal man into a fit.

So that means I was able to believe his description of the girl in the restaurant. Early twenties. Intelligent forehead. Natural, well-shaped eyebrows. Unpredictable eyes. Lovely nose with gypsy nostrils. A full, unwrinkled mouth. Good breasts. At least the right one, which was all he could see because of where he was sitting and because her boy friend was blocking the left. All that was left were the legs, which of course he couldn't see, but with the rest of her the way it was, he'd go for the legs sight unseen.

To get that would be impossible, he thought, because for all Will's charm, he had been known to come away with the twenty-second best looking girl in a room. So he thought he'd just sit there, have a bowl of wonton soup and startle her into looking at him, at least, while the other lucky bastard would get to close the deal.

The waitress arrived and threw the menu down in front of Will. He pointed to number five and she left him to get on with his crazy lovemaking.

So far she wasn't noticing, and he'd already burnt three matches, having inserted them alight into his gaping mouth —but she caught the fourth one, and a good one it was. The pretty girl waited, and Will knew he had her attention for as long as he kept it in there, which in this case was a bit too long. But anything for the cause. He removed it, grinned his famous grin, and she turned away with not the slightest change in expression. Could it be that she wasn't looking at him at all?

The chunky, red haired (braided), freckled waitress arrived again with the wonton soup. And while she was there, filled the sugar jar—interfering very much with his act.

By now, he looked so ridiculous trying to look past the moving arms and bobbing head of the waitress that he did, in fact, have the pretty girl laughing. He picked up a fork and jabbed his cheek. Not because it was funny but out of panic, and the very fact that he was trying so hard must have been impressing her.

He wore his chopsticks between his top lip and his nose, Ubangi-style, placed a lit cigarette across his open palm, slapped his wrist, with the intention of having it land tip first in his mouth. (It landed behind the cash register.) Threw things in the air, crossed his eyes—everything imaginable that might keep her amused. But never, never in a thousand years did he ever hope to have her look at him the way she finally did. That was when her boy friend slipped off to the washroom.

Will stopped his foolish-face act and looked straight through her, counting for the first time on his mother's sensitive but strong presence, and his father's eyes. I'll be goddamned if it didn't work. She returned his careless, interested look with a careless, interested look of her own. Even the odd-looking and irritatingly bad-mannered waitress didn't bother them, as she rattled dishes, wiped the table, slammed down his coffee and scratched her left cheek.

The girl was his. He knew it. Never had he pulled it off so smoothly.

Now to be patient and wait for her sign. The friend would be coming out of the washroom and paying the cheque. She probably had already written a fast note and would drop it on the table as she went by. "Holy jumpin'! Dis is workin' real good," said Will to himself.

The friend came out of the washroom, and they started on their way up the aisle. She'd have to throw him the note now. "Shit!" Maybe she didn't want to take the chance on throwing it. Maybe she didn't write it, was even a better guess, but she sure as hell wouldn't be back. "Holy Dyin'!" thought Will.

He still had to put in another ten minutes while the waitress changed and picked up her pay. He walked almost frantically back-and-forth on the wet sidewalk, hoping like hell that he'd see something better before the ten minutes were up. But it was as if every woman in town knew what he was thinking and stayed off the streets purposely.

So with his head on a pillow, and an arm behind his neck, his eyes open and a smile on his face, he indulged in his very favourite pastime: erotic recall—and not necessarily for the pretty one who got away, but also for the strange-looking off–duty waitress lying just far enough over on the bed to make the whole thing pleasantly memorable. As a matter of fact, after she had unbraided her hair, brushed it out, and turned out all the lights (Will wished that he could get at the lamps on the sidewalk too), she wasn't as terrible as all that.

The only other thing was her voice. Will made her a small bet that she couldn't get through the whole thing without talking. Once she did say "Oh Will," and he had to start pretending that she was the pretty girl all over again.

"Will," she cooed from the other side of the bed.

"Yeah?"

"Feel okay?"

"Lovely, tell your mother. Wasn't it lovely?"

"Oh yes." She shifted her head to his shoulder, rearranging her hair, which all landed neatly across Will's face like a great fan of shredded rope.

He tucked it all down between them and worried for a second about the possibilities of seconds, but only for a second. Then he threw the whole idea out as a terrible one.

"Want me to stay tonight?" he asked, and unseen by her, made an awful face at the very thought. But she surprised and delighted him.

"Oh, God no! You can't stay all night. My parents will kill me!"

Her reaction launched Will into an act of protest, the drama of which he enjoyed so much that he took far too long getting into his clothes and away from there.

"Holy jumpin'," he started. "Ya take what ya want and

t'row me out. Dat it? I know. I'm just on me way t'rough, but I'm used to better treatment dan dat, y'know. How d'ya tink dat makes me feel, if dat's all I'm wort' to ya—all right. A *one-nighter* for Chris' sake!"

She had been trying to get a word in. "No. That's not it —but I'd get holy hell if you stayed here all night." Although she was glad he mentioned it.

Will's balance wasn't too good at the best of times and he bounced off a wall, getting into his pants. "Ah-h-h-h-h bloody girls—"

"Will, for God's sake."

"What?"

"Not so loud, please."

"I'm tryin' to get to me boots. Is dere a light in dis place?"

"No, they'll see a light. Just feel your way."

"What d'ya tink I've been doin'? For hours. Where da hell is it? Oh, here it is."

He finally got to the door. "I s'pose ya don't even know da name of a good hotel."

"A—let's see—"

"I t'ought so," he said, and with jacket and one boot on and his overnight case in his hands, he walked heavily to the door, flung it open and barged through the dark house to the front door, leaving a panic-stricken girl behind on the bed.

I can imagine her mouth opening wide and nothing coming forth as she listened to a chair falling over, then a lamp, and finally the door slamming.

It must have been bloody uncomfortable, sitting on the wet front steps, tucking in his shirt, and getting ready to leave, and a hell of a bore when the upstairs window came open.

"Hey! Who the hell are you?" the father screamed.

"Doctor Smit'. Just makin' a house call. She's goin' to be all right," and he removed himself from the front step, and travelled for about two blocks with one boot on and one flopping wet sock.

He had seen better times.

RUTH LOWE

There was nothing he ever said that obligated him, and nothing he ever did that involved him knowingly in my *private,* perfect plan of a life together. He was involved no deeper than he had been involved in my dreams as a six-teen-year-old. And even those were dreams that started when I was still awake:

"My name is Ruth—What's yours?"

I imagined I was meeting Will for the first time, and that he was the kindest, most perfect young man I'd ever met, and he thought I was perfect too, which made it all lovely:

"Oh, am I? Am I really pretty?"

It was easy to see that everything the young man said he meant, which made me feel safe. That was so important. Knowing that kind of thing was what made me take his hand when he offered it and, even at ten, my imaginary Will didn't care what the other boys thought of him. He was too much of a man to feel silly, so by doing what he wanted to do he made the others look up to him. And guess what! I believed my mother loved him, and so did my father. So did I, and so did everyone, because in my dreams he was the most perfect boy in town.

The most perfect boy in town. Was that what *I* wanted? No, that was what my *mother* wanted.

Will did the running-away-from-home that I never got around to. My liberating force from a life of too much dot-ing. Being called perfect all the time, I never believed I could do anything, so that even when I began to do things of my very own with my own creative juices, which would, I'm sure, have brought something, anything worthwhile, to the top, I was too busy questioning myself to allow anything to happen naturally. So, rather than try and fail, I took a trip down to the store with my mother and bought yet another pretty dress.

Similarly, whenever she saw I was getting restless, she'd suggest I'd go to a movie (which was her answer for me at times when she thought I needed a little excitement and romance in my life). Did she think that slopping up love on the silver screen would serve my need for passionate abandonment? Was a monthly trip to the Popular Theatre supposed to fill and re-fill that secret, cursed, lady's void already overflowing with the hoardings of my curious, though distorted, imaginings?

And didn't I know anyone? she'd asked.

Lots and lots of people, but they didn't know me very well.

"Would you like us to entertain more?"

"No, thank you, mom."

I think I must have been twenty-three when she began to worry that the wavy-haired, pipe-smoking gentleman in the smart-looking, red satin smoking jacket from our Simpson–Sears catalogue would not come.

I wanted Will as he was and as he is. I was afraid that if I didn't want him that way, I'd never get him. Well, I supposed I'd never really have him for my own, and it's that negative kind of thinking that made up my later dreams. Not dreams, but *dream*. Just one.

"I don't know you. You shouldn't say those things to me," I fantasized.

But even at a young age, his imperfections were somehow strangely appealing to me. Probably because he got away with things. He was his own young man even then, and already independent; and if he wasn't allowed to be, the big people would know it.

That is the kind of courage I would never have, I thought, as I would struggle to remain within the dream a little longer. But inevitably, my mother's call from the bottom of the stairs, for school, would put an end to it, and I would be forced to trade my dreamland Will, (much more pliable and attentive) for the schoolroom Will (arrogant and indifferent). As demanding as these attitudes were upon my patience, I could never alter my thinking of him (which I've thought since was a pretty classy facet of my own character, thank you very much), and could certainly never influence

100

the inevitable outcome of my TV serial-type dream. I looked forward to its continuation:

"I'm a good girl. I'm good."

This Will was more authentic than my young imagined prince and had his mind made up that *his* word was *law*. But I didn't want to lose him. I didn't. There were lots who were waiting. I don't know, I am a good girl, and it wouldn't mean anything to him one way or the other. But it would to me, wouldn't it? To know I was with him. Wanted by him. Pleasing to him and pleased by him. Just don't laugh at me and snap your fingers at me. I need to know it means something to you—

"Does it Will? Are you going away now? No, don't. Not yet. I'm sorry I'm so stupid about it."

Go away mother, I thought. So I won't have to see you in the morning. I know it's only a dream, but I'd rather you weren't down in the kitchen when the serial comes to an end. I'm sixteen and I need him. I'm sorry. I have to be faithful to myself and to where I want the dream to end. It goes on—

"Will you?—please?—No, I haven't—ever—Will you? I won't cry out—I'll be very quiet."

Voices? Am I still in the dream? Or are they coming through the hot air register? Sometimes that happens. But it's all right—

"Please—please—I don't even know how. I don't know what it's like—please. Yes. I'm asking. Now—now—you can't go. You can't. Stay. Stay. Stay . . ."

It was no longer Mom's voice that broke the dream and made him go away. It was my own and that was much, much worse, because to my way of thinking it meant I might always be living according to someone else's rules and wishes all my life.

* * * * *

That dream was, after all those years and into the unkind reality of my thirties, played out to the end, at the picnic. The Fox Farm again. Ideal for church picnics. There were hills and trails, a playground for kids, enough flat ground

101

for fifty small groups of picnickers and the slowly shifting river going on behind it all, carrying its colourful boats and their weekend sailors. And the forest. I had my thoughts about the forest, but that could wait while I helped get things organized for Reverend Perry.

It was pretty though. There was an abundance of pastel shades. Dresses, hats, men's white shirts, and the brilliant green of the field. Renoir is whose work it always reminded me of, not God's at all (with apologies to Reverend Perry).

It dawned on me that at last year's picnic and at this one, there were very few in my age bracket. The majority were older, or there were the kids who were already taking part in their games. But I refused to read anything into it. I felt pretty good. I had just washed my hair, and the new slack suit that Mom and Dad brought me back from their trip to Montreal was perfect for the occasion, as long as I was careful what I sat on. So I thought I looked just right. In case. In case of what? What in the name of heaven was I thinking about, and had been thinking about since I first spread out the family's blanket, thereby staking our claim for the picnic in our favourite spot of all. But why should I have been thinking about it? Why was I so absolute positive that it had been Will I had seen running back and forth down at the far end of the field.

Dad's pipe, tobacco and pipe cleaners were neatly spread out on one corner of the blanket.

"This was a good idea," Dad said.

"Yes, wasn't it," my Mom replied. Then sitting up, shading her eyes with her one hand, she pointed to the sky.

"What kind of birds are they, Jack?"

"I believe they're Turrs," he said. "I haven't had a good feed of Turrs since Harold Tulk brought us that half-dozen in from Gander two years ago."

They asked me where I was going. "Just around," I said. "Carol Tilley is down there somewhere. I'm going to try and find her."

"Carol Tilley. Do I know her?" asked my mother.

"Tilleys on Polygon Road—Claire and Ron," my father answered.

I mentioned that she was a steady of Andrew Scott's.

"Him," she remembered with some distaste. Not because she knew that much about him, but because he had been an associate of "that Will Cole person."

"That's one fellow who'd better not show his nose at this affair," she said with great authority.

To tell her that he'd already shown his nose would have brought on a seizure or sent her packing, so instead of mentioning it, I left for the other end of the field and into the world of the games, cotton candy, school girls' band, broad jumps, high jumps, three-legged races and tug-o-wars. The tug-o-war was going on when I arrived, and among the contestants were Constable Williams (uniform and all) and Andrew.

"Look at him," said Carol, who had appeared out of nowhere. "He won't be satisfied till Mr. Williams is flat on his uniform in that pool of mud between them. Oh my God, look! Williams's boot went in!"

But he got it back out and, just as Andrew's team gave the winning tug, Williams quit the rope and jumped to one side, saving himself the embarrassment of messing up his uniform.

"Where's Will?" Williams asked Andrew.

"He's hiding behind me," said Andrew.

Williams made a sound like that of an old barn door opening, and rolled away. But not before he could say to Andrew and Carol, "An' no more of that kissin', you an' her. Before you know it, you'll cause a bloody epidemic."

He left them laughing, as I cagily scanned the area for Will. Andrew couldn't wait to tell the Williams conversation to Will, so he too, began to look around.

"Hey! Will."

He found him! Will heard, and without looking, waved at Andrew's voice and ran into the woods, laughing. Andrew sensed my look of bewilderment, turned away and pretended to be occupied.

What would have made him run like that? It couldn't have been a rabbit? He didn't have a gun. Oh, I knew. To do "you-know-what." But laughing? Then, having given him

103

that many "outs," I settled on what I always thought to be the true motive. He was chasing a girl.

When I saw her, I almost breathed a sigh of relief. I'm not one to be catty, but she was not my type, and she was not the English actress. (Mary told me about her.) She was definitely the kind of girl who would run around in the woods with a man while she was thinking about how else to entertain him. In her case she would not come up with an alternative and that would be it.

I felt sorry for her and interested in her predicament. Enough so, that I decided to create a diversion for her until she got out of the woods, so to speak. But if I caught my new pants suit on a twig, Will Cole would certainly know about it.

Well, I might as well admit it. I think I must have become temporarily insane. Not just because I'd strolled away from my family's picnic blanket, and all the decency and wholesomeness and tradition that went with it, and marched straight into the woods; but because all I had been had suddenly become unreal, and I was admitting that that freckled, wild–haired, overweight, bra–less, Sunday afternoon jungle girl had more fun out of one afternoon without thinking about it than I'd had in my total, crosslegged life. I'm sure that that is why I feel the way I do about weekends. With every Friday paycheck, there came two more days of thumb twiddling before I could again resume my sensational career as a smiling bank teller. But this girl must have loved weekends. "HURRAY! FORTY EIGHT HOURS TO RUN THROUGH THE WOODS!"

What could *I* have been in search of, in case I was asked? Berries? Old rocks? Indian bones? Sea shells? No. I *knew* what I was searching for, and I was suddenly very, very sorry for myself. I *deserved* better. I deserved much better than this.

I spotted her great, pumpkin-face coming through the trees. Listen to me. Great pumpkin-face. I'd never been that honest about anyone's appearance in my sweet life. No, it wasn't even honest, it was cruel. I *felt* cruel, and I was beginning to like it a bit. At least until I would be shown some attention by someone. Sometime. Anytime.

So there she was. She could have been a moose, the way she came charging through there. Being a fine woodswoman she knew just how to get those trees out of her way so that no harm would come to her already–injured–but–laughing face and her abnormally heavy and unfortunately low-slung chest.

Her feet were bare (which made sense) and her toenails needed trimming and she had cavities and her hair needed washing, and there were lots of other things I could mention if I'd taken time–out from my berrypicking. She passed on through my small clearing and broke a new trail through to the west.

That incredible looking girl was not to be outdone by the incredible looking man that followed. So *that* was what the devil looked like up close. His shirt was wide open, his hair, wet and stringy, covered his face to his laughing mouth, his glistening neck was as red as a Christmas apple, and his arms and chest were covered with bleeding scratches.

How he could laugh while being slapped with those swishing branches, I'll never know; and of course he would have been spared a lot of that if he had been a good woodsman. But Will never was.

He hurtled right on by me and returned instantly. As shocked as he was to see me, he was too busy gasping and wheezing to say anything but, 'Wha—wha—wha—' but he finally finished it. "What are you doin' in such a place?"

"What do you mean 'such a place'? Sure we're having a church picnic up at the other end."

"Church? Hee-hee-ee. Is dat what all dat is about? Who's idea was dat?"

"Reverend Perry. He came with us."

I thought he was going to die between his laughing and coughing.

"Well I hope he ain't planned a trek t'rough the woods, or he'll step on a few people who didn't go to church dis morning."

"You're joking, Will."

"I am not. These bushes are loaded. Yer picnic is surrounded. Sure, ya've been here, haven't ya?"

"I have not. Never." I answered truthfully, and almost disgusted that he ever mentioned it.

"No, but you must've known about it. Come on now."

"No!" which was a small lie.

"Oh," said the madman. "Funny though, idden it?" and he was off again in stitches.

I told him that it was not a bit funny and that his girl friend would get away.

"Nah. She won't notice I'm gone for anodder half-hour yet. Who is she anyway?"

"Who is she?" I was almost laughing myself. "Don't you know who she is?"

"No. She grabbed me by the shirt a few minutes ago out on the road—tore it too, look—den she took off, so I took off after her. I been chasin' 'er for a jeezley long time. She can run, whoever she is."

"You're a crazyman."

We stopped and listened to what sounded like the girl's voice. Yes. That was her all right, and she was calling *him*.

He got itchy and told me to go back to my folks. I told him I didn't want to go. He asked me why not. I wanted to sit here and talk to him; I told him, quite aware of the ants in his pants.

"Look. I got to go, anyway," he said.

"Not yet. Talk to me for awhile, for heaven's sake. You'd think I was going to hurt you."

"Never know. We've heard about you."

We strolled into pleasanter surroundings, and it was nice. And I was grateful for the comfortable understanding we'd always had about each other. Nothing dangerous. Nothing dirty. Just a rare communicative thing that has always been very important and necessary to me. In that area, at least, I was pretty certain I was valuable to him.

"How's old Andrew doin' out dere?" he asked.

Before I could answer, he was shouting in the girl's direction. "YA'D BETTER GET GOIN'. I'M COUNTIN' TO T'REE AN' I'M COMIN' IN!"

I answered, almost deafened by an earful of his sharp voice. "He's okay. He's with Carol."

"Yeah, I know. The wedding is soon, so he's not movin' around too much. You still at da bank?"

I told him I was and that I'd be there till I was eighty.

"Dat's not too far off is it? Look, what d'ya tink people would say if dey saw ya in the bushes like dis, *wit' me,* wha?"

"They'd say: 'Oh look! There goes clean old Ruth and dirty old Will.'"

He laughed hard, and it always made me feel especially good when he found me funny that way. Then, he took the only berry I'd found out of the palm of my hand and threw it into his big mouth. "Tanks."

"WILL!!!" (It was the girl again.) He asked me if I had any secrets to tell him.

"Lots! Good ones too, but why should I tell them to *you?*" I said.

We'd been standing up till then, 'cause I didn't care to mess up my new pants suit if it only meant hello and good-bye, thank you very much. (If anyone I knew even thought I thought thoughts like that, they'd excommunicate me on the spot. Or be amused. I don't know which.)

"Look at dat perfect six-by-four-foot space over dere by da alders," he said, with a lot of meaning. "Want to know what went on dere?"

"I know."

"Some educated, you are, den."

Before I knew it, I'd taken the old baseball out of my jacket pocket and held it up for him to see.

"What've ya got dere, maid?"

"Baseball."

It came to him and he was truly delighted.

"Oh, my God. You still got dat old ting?" he laughed, and I self–consciously tucked it away again until he asked to see it. (I could hardly look at him—isn't that odd for a girl my age?)

"Sure, it's fallin' apart. Look at it!" he said.

"I know," and I was suddenly concerned that it's innards were falling out. I tucked them back in and held it tight.

"Guess ya'll have to tape it," he said.

"I guess so." I don't know for sure, but I had the feeling it meant something to him too. Even if only because it once belonged to him.

"Is it the same ball, Will?"

He assured me that it was, in fact, the same ball that Garfield Day and he had been throwing back and forth that long-ago day on this same Fox Farm, while Will's eldest sister, Hilda, looked on.

* * * * *

Garfield's car was a 1942 Plymouth and it was covered in dust from his early morning trip to the town of Botwood. His sister opened a few bottles of Orange Crush and put out a few sandwiches on a pale green blanket, I remember. (I had left my family and was sauntering by, by accident.)

"Look Will!" his sister said.

He looked around. "What?"

"I see comeone." Her voice was sing-songy.

"Who? Who?"

"Over there by the trees. Look!"

He saw me and turned away immediately.

"Why don't you go over and see her?"

"Sure, what for? Holy dyin'."

"You won't have to," said Garfield. "Here she comes to see you."

Will got panicky and tried to prevent any such confrontation from happening, so he ran out into the field in the opposite direction.

"HEY, GAR, T'ROW US A CATCH!" and Gar threw it all right but more in my direction and at an unfair rate of speed. Will ran and leaped for it but he just wasn't tall enough to handle it, so it sailed past him, dropped, and bounced along through the grass. I walked towards it.

Will took on his usual look of panic whenever he saw me and burrowed madly through the grass in search of the ball. We hadn't even said hello.

108

"I think it's further over this way towards that old log." I said.

"No, it's in here. I saw it land. Here it is." He could have been talking to a field mouse for all that he looked at me, but I was happy that it was he that found it. Not that I really tried.

"You found it. You were right." I said, smiling. I looked pretty. I had on my white pique with the pale mauve ribbon woven through the neck and waist, and knee socks.

Will looked pretty too. Even though his little faded shirt had a frayed collar and was half tucked in and half out. His blue pants were his first and most recent pair, and his brave little boots—that had served as his skate boots (bound to the skate with wire or rope), ski boots (bound to barrel staves), and his everyday walking boots. (The ankles wore out almost as soon as the bottoms, because Will had learned to walk that way. Even now, his feet are not his most handsome feature. They look as though they'd been on Napoleon's winter march from Moscow and had not survived.) Oh, and he had on his brother Lon's cap.

He gripped the ball, after banging it into his hand with vein-bursting force (because that's what Lou and Babe and his other bubblegum–player–card friends did), called to Gar and sent it flying back to him. He was satisfied with his sister's choice of Gar. "He drives a taxi. We came in his car. Look at 'er."

"Yes, it's nice," I said. "Is he going to marry your sister?"

"I hope so. Den I could come here all da time."

"Do you have a snap that I could have for my album?" I was getting brave, but I didn't really expect one.

He made a face. "A snap! No, I don' have a snap."

"Not even an old one? Maybe your sister would have one of you if I asked her."

He was getting close to a shout. "No. She don't have one eider. No snaps! What d'ya want a snap for?"

"I just want one. I got lots at home. Just for souvenirs, that's all."

"Haven't got one. No one's got one. Not takin' any."

His sister and her friend were ready to go. They waved,

109

and Gar threw him the ball one last time. Will caught it. I think he hurt his finger.

"Goin' now." and he left. In an unbelievably daring moment, I ran up to him, snatched the ball out of his hand and headed for my father's car. He started to chase after me but the sight of my family stopped him.

"HEY! GIMME DAT!" he screeched. "IT'S DA ONLY ONE I GOT."

But I kept running until I was locked safely inside the car.

* * * * *

"Dat was da only one I had, too," he repeated twenty-four years later on our patch of grass close by the picnic; and he threatened to grab it, but I was too fast for him.

"If I wanted it, I'd take it," he said. It was a very heavy moment that followed.

"I'm sure you would." I said, and looked beyond his grey-green eyes for his next reaction. He refused to take part in my game of double meanings, which I was sorry I ever started because I had that feeling again, that every time I did or said something that was not expected of Ruth Lowe, I was bordering on prostitution. I felt suddenly sad, as I looked at the ball.

"I don't suppose it'll be the same ball if I tape it over, will it?"

"Sure it will. Don't be so foolish, girl. The outside'll be new, but the inside'll be the same as it always was."

I felt better immediately.

"HEY!" It was *her* voice again, but not any closer, which made me think that the poor thing wasn't the navigator I'd given her credit for.

"Hee-hee-eee, she's still roamin' around in dere." said Will and kicked his legs in the air, until change for a dollar fell out of his pocket. "Are there any new boy friends you want to tell me about?"

"No," I said, "and there won't be any. I'm going into a convent."

"Yes, you'd make some sister, brudder."

110

"I might as well." There I go again. Coming on too strong. I was bound to get into trouble that way.

"Get out of it. Convent."

"Or a nice home—in the new development—lots of babies—"

He laughed again. "You'll get dem soon enough, if ya keeps takin' your walks in dese woods."

"HEY! WHERE ARE YA WILL? WILL-L-L-L!"

I never knew my secret prince's name could sound so wrong for him. Will stood up for this one. "I'M COMIN' NOW. ONE!" Then, "I'm goin' for a beer, Root."

"We all know where you're going."

The look on his face was nice, as he stood there, grinning, but looking at me for the first time. Then he walked over to where I was sitting and was so close that his fingers touched my hair, and I shivered—and kept right on shivering. But instead of feeling confident, instead of feeling as divine as I did when I started out the day, I felt awkward as hell. You know how it feels to try on a dress and find it's much too big. You like it, and you want it to work, but the shoulder seems keep slipping down your arms, making you feel tiny and shapeless, like the little match girl. That was it. Shapeless and undesirable.

At this point his voice sounded diffcrent. "Good old Root."

"HEY!" that damned girl shouted, away off somewhere.

"TWO." said Will looking straight at me.

"Bad old Will." I whispered. He touched my hair again and took his fingers away again.

"Root. Sometime—just once—we should—"

"Should what?"

"Put in a little time together—just for the fun of it."

"We've spent time together, what do you mean?"

"Not the kind of time I'm talkin' about."

"I didn't think you had any time left over."

"An' I didn't tink you'd go along—" He touched me again, and I brought my fingers up slowly and very gently touched his chin. Then I took them away again.

"You've always been afraid of me," I said.

"Not me, brudder." But he was, you know.

111

"Then what's been wrong?" By now, I was being very helpful, and not wanting to be.

"You know what's wrong. We know each other."

Why did he say that? It won't happen, I could feel it. It would end like the dream. In nothingness. I would be incomplete again, and my life would be incomplete. There's nothing to me. There's a dull, boring nothingness to the way I looked, the way I was, the way I could always expect to be. If I were a problem, there'd be no solution. If I were a question, I'd be unanswerable.

But even so—don't breathe—and who knows what may happen? If you blink your eyes, he'll change his mind. How's that for insecurity? Don't breathe. Oh my God, I'm sure I had onion in my mother's egg sandwiches. Don't breathe. Wait and see—you can wait one more second or two—

He spoke. "I just don't know if I can be right." He was softer than I could ever have imagined. Softer and gentler than he'd been in my hundred–year–old dream.

He moved away an inch or two, but returned. He looked as though he was thinking, "But we're friends." I've never sat so still. I was right. He won't be able to touch me. He feels funny about it all. I look odd to him.

I took his hand. I didn't care anymore who started what or at what precise second. I placed it on my breast, and could feel the breeze escape between our faces when I moistened my lips. (*Oh God, don't moisten your lips!*) But if I didn't, he would have thought I was wrinkly and crinkly like the old maid that I was getting close to being; besides I don't think he saw, and even if he did, he couldn't have worried about it because he kissed me.

When we parted for the first time and looked at each other, I understood, if only for that sweet moment or two or for however long the afternoon would last, who Ruth Lowe was, and why she was, and why, of all the people in the world, she was with him.

Somehow, too, I felt tremendously victorious, and felt so long after the picnic noises ended, long after our first kiss and long after my honourable female opponent had caused

112

the ground to shake around us, with what was to be the final cry of anguish in her terrible defeat:
"YOU DIDN'T SAY THREE!!!"

*   *   *   *   *

I seem to remember when I liked chocolate. Especially at Easter when, since money was no particular object, my father would get me the biggest chocolate bunny in the store. And they were heavy and solid and really all that a bunny should be.

Then one year my mother, for the good of my teeth, cut down on sweets, and Easter was particularly affected. Because the next time I opened a basket, I found, not my usual heavy bunny, but a nothing bunny. "Oh well, at least it'll be solid." and of course, you know, it wasn't.

And neither was Will. I watched from the bank window as usual. The truck arrived, Will and Andrew piled out, Andrew met Carol on the corner and they walked up a side street. That left Will.

He stopped to light a cigarette and continued up the opposite sidewalk. I know I was expectant, and I suppose I shouldn't have been. I smiled. He smiled. I waved. He waved. And that was about all we could have done. He stopped, gave a slight shrug to his shoulders and smiled: *I'm sorry, that's about all there was to it. Yesterday afternoon was great, but not quite great enough. You were lovely, tell your mother, but not quite lovely enough, and not experienced enough, not nearly enough for the grown-ups—that* sort of smile.

(Don't be foolish. He wasn't thinking those things. That's not what the shrug meant at all. He's as beautiful as ever. He simply wants to save you before it's too late.)

I still wanted to scream at myself until my throat hurt: "What are you standing in this window for. You won't have to perch up here anymore, and let your tea get cold."

He shoved his hands in his pockets, and, partially shielded by shoppers, he made his way up the sidewalk, probably figuring out tomorrow's route home, reached his street and disappeared; and I relaxed and felt myself go pale. I'd lost my gamble.

I saw him next at Andrew's wedding.

ANDREW SCOTT

I suppose I began to notice it after his last trip to St. John's. The stories he told seemed forced, somehow. Or, to be more accurate, they were created or re-created to serve as a kind of report on what he knew I'd expect from him.

He seemed relieved that the stories satisfied me. Only then could he rid himself of the episode entirely. In fact, he gave me the feeling that he would never go back to St. John's again.

I don't know why the attitude bothered me. It certainly wasn't because he was down. In fact, he was even more *Will* than he'd ever been, if that's possible. More laughter, more swagger, more bounce. Even the slamming of a door was slightly more than before. I won't say exaggerated, because you might take that to mean unnatural—but I do *mean* that, although most other people wouldn't notice.

Here's something else. Although Will swallowed up life in large quantities, he was amazingly unlike that when he ate and drank. He just *looked* as though he would gobble and gulp like a gut-foundered lumberjack, but he was the reverse—until this change that I'm talking about. Now, there isn't enough beer or salt beef in town.

The change, whatever had done it, was worth noticing and thinking about, even if the stimulus of it would always remain a secret. I knew one thing. He was now doing enough living for two men.

Of course, this wasn't exactly a dull time for me either. Carol and me were inching our way, steadily and nervously, towards the wedding; that's if I didn't run away before. What was there about it after all that made it so frightening to me? Growing up, I guess.

I suddenly remembered old Frank Downs and the wife and nine kids. No, by God, TEN. They had one more now. Well, the only thing that prevented Frank from chucking it all and becoming a missing person was his gut. His gut was where all his fat was. The rest of him wasn't worth talking

115

about. But you know what? that little round gut, as long as it was filled, was a reminder of his security at home. He could always expect to have his little round gut as long as he toed the line, but (and she made this clear) he wouldn't last a day out there in the world without it.

I had a lot to think about. I picked up a bag of hamburgers and chips in the store across the road from Will's place and met him at the gate, and we started on our free afternoon's walk to anywhere. Will, who couldn't sit still for a second anyway, was glad to go. Of course, it's like having a cheetah on a leash. Especially that day, which happened to be at the end of the picnic week, and after I'd first suspected a kind of odd something or other in his and Ruth's friendship.

They never ever spent any time together hardly, but at least they had a good laugh whenever they did; which didn't happen when the four of us met two days before our walk. Carol and Ruth were talky enough, but Will kept wanting to get away, and Ruth noticed it too, I believe.

Will didn't look like Will when he frowned, and he sure as hell did a lot of it during our stroll.

"Did you want onions?" I asked, as I saw him pry the tinfoil off his hamburger.

"No."

"That's too bad."

He pulled out the onion rings, slapped them into my waiting palm and went for his chips.

"Where are the plastic forks?" he asked.

"In the shagging store." I said.

"Can't send ya for anyting."

"That's for sure."

We'd just passed the high school when he asked for his other hamburger. I removed the onion and tossed it to him. I felt like talking.

"Know how long I've known Carol? That's what I was thinking on my way over to see you. Know how long? Not long. I knew who she was, but I never knew her."

He grunted.

"And you know what? They lived next door to us for years.

116

On Polygon. I never knew that. Did you? That they lived on Polygon? In a green house, she said. Then they moved to Circular Road where they are now. And you know where I met her? Guess."

I could tell by his second grunt that he didn't want to guess.

"At the rink about eight years ago. A game between the Rovers and the Rink Rats. Bill Hall was killed right after that. Remember? Ran into a train. Some good in defence, he was, Jesus, I just thought of it! Porky Ryan and Bram White were in the same car. That's right! And Bram had just lost his father two weeks before. His sister Joyce was all right to look at though, brother. Hey, know who's something to look at? That one there."

I pointed to a woman leaning up against a tree and talking to young Slaps Andrews, who looked like he was trying something with her. She was saucy looking enough to be a Cobb. In fact, she could've been "Gob" Cobb, but she died of cancer a little over a year ago. Her real name was Donna. We called her "Gob" because she had these great big lips and talked a lot. I believe it was cancer. I'm not sure. Anyway, I pointed to her.

"Too old." said Will.

"Go on," I said, "There's nothing in Newfoundland too old for you."

We didn't intend walking all the way to the waterfall, but we were headed that way.

"Did you know my brother Cec got his moose? He also knows a lot about plumbing, did you know that? That'll come in handy when Carol and me are moved into our own place. First the family said, 'Come and live with us. Won't cost you anything.' But I couldn't take that. Not with the way Cec's wife goes on. Talk? My Jesus, can that woman talk. And cry? Can she cry! Hey, I know someone you got to meet. I just thought of it. Carol's sister, Sharon. You'd like her, brother. Some nice, she is. Great legs. Better than Carol. Don't tell Carol. Yes, by God, you've got to meet that one. I never met her but from what Carol says, she's the real beauty in the family. She's in Boston."

117

Will stopped right there and looked at me. "Well, what did ya tell me about her for, when she's in the States?"

"I don't know."

"No, dat's what ya don't." he said.

I waited till he wanted to say something, which was a long, long time.

"Who's yer best man goin' ta be?"

"Prince Philip. What're you talking about? Who's my best man!"

"I s'pose dat means I got to get a tie," said Will.

"I'll bring one, in case you forget."

I kept on walking and talking, my mouth getting dry for some reason, and didn't realize I'd left him standing looking at the waterfall, but there he was. Now, he'd seen that old thing often enough not to have to stop and study it like that. When he'd had enough of it, he walked right on by me and led the way. I watched him.

You know, I'm not a conceited man but it ran through my head that afternoon that Will would be greatly affected by my getting married. I'm sure he wondered what he would do on his own.

Then, guess what? He reached into his back pocket and pulled out—can you guess? An old, homemade catapult. A CATAPULT! By working the handle, he twirled the rubber straps around his fingers, and while he was looking around for stones, I just hung there staring at him.

"What the hell is that?" I asked him.

He was amazed at my ignorance.

"Catapult."

"I know it's a catapult. What're you doing with it?"

"Nothing. It's mine. I made it years ago. It was broke and I fixed it, dat's all."

He continued this childishness by combing the grass on his hands and knees for ammunition. "Find me some rocks now. Nice, juicy, small round ones."

"Find them yourself, I got to meet Carol." I figured I'd get away from him before he got me into a game of hide and seek. He stopped me.

"Andrew."

118

"Yeah."

"We've tied a few on haven't we?"

"That's what we have, my son."

"Good times."

"A few, sir."

"Hang'er down a second. Hang 'er down."

I stopped, but he was having a great deal of trouble with whatever it was he was trying to say.

"Hey Andrew—ya know how everyone goes on about me —'bout da way I acts da fool?"

"Yeah." And here he had great surprise in his voice, as though he'd just discovered he was illegitimate.

"Dey've never liked dat, y'know."

I couldn't do much more than to feel sorry for him, which I did, a great deal.

"Why don't dey, do ya tink?"

"I don't know."

He moved away. For whatever reason he said it to me, it was important not to let him think about it too long.

"Know what I did yesterday?" I asked. "Put our names down for an electrician's course."

"Mine, too?" he asked.

"Yeah."

"What did ya do dat for?"

"Getting fed up on the job. I want to do something else. Especially now that I'm getting married, y'know."

"OK, but why'd ya put my name down?"

"It'll do you good. Use your head for a change. You've got brains, you dumb bastard."

He gave me the long steady burn of an older man. The kind that always made him look different, somehow.

"Well, Andrew, when ya goes by dere again, scratch mine out, will ya, like a good b'y?"

I insisted that he could get through it laughing, but he didn't hear me. Whatever else he was thinking about sure made him happier than he'd been all afternoon. He gave me a fake punch in the gut and kept searching for his small, juicy, round stones.

"There's a whole bunch of them," I said, pointing into the

119

grass. And as soon as he was well bent over, I gave him a lash with my boot and took off towards the slope that dipped into town. I looked around just once, to see him scramble for a stone to shoot me with. He shouted that he'd found one and came running like a mad thing. But only for a few yards. And he didn't shoot me with it after all.

*   *   *   *   *

He had his curious-contented face on that night when he arrived at Moore's Restaurant-Bakeshop, and was boozy enough to get himself into trouble straight away.

He felt like a pie. That's what he wanted! A big hefty pie and a bottle of beer. Lemon pie, too, by God—and a hand of poker to go along with it. Knowing he could get all of that out at the back in the bakeshop, he headed straight on through the restaurant section, got a light from old Mr. Cooper in the last booth, and entered through the swinging bakery doors to where Pat Lane was banging away on a slab of dough and Jim Rubie and one of the Anthony brothers from Monchy road were deep into "Jacks."

Having given Anthony's hand a look, Will told Jim Rubie not to be so foolish; then when he got a look at Jim's hand, he told him to go ahead, and they all got upset.

"Hello dere, Pat." said Will with more than enough friendship in his voice. Pat didn't answer. Pat doesn't most of the time. That's why he's Pat Lane and not anyone else.

"Any extras, old man?" asked Will, as he pored over the tarts and pies.

"No," snapped Pat. "None. No more free pies, an' Mr. Moore says no one is allowed back here anymore."

"I'm some hungry, one pie an' I'll go."

"No. Nothing atall. No pies and no tarts. Nothing. No sir."

I had just sopped up the last of what was a bloody good attempt at a stew that Carol had put together at her folks' place, when my friend called from the bake shop. Carol took it and started answering Will's questions about how the plans were going.

"Fine," she said. "But you know, Will, I never really thought I'd be nervous. Everyone's nervous, but I thought I had it beat until this afternoon when it all started up in my stomach.

"Well, dat's reasonable," said my friend. "You should be nervous, too. Didn't he tell ya? Someone give 'im da boot in a fight when he was fifteen. He's been out of commission for years, m'dear."

I heard his squeal of laughter from where I was sitting in the other room.

"Oh, don't be foolish," said Carol and gave the phone to me.

"What did you tell her?"

"Nothing you'd want to hear. Come on out for a fast beer, now. Unlucky to be in tonight."

"No boy, got to stay in shape. We'll have one after the wedding though."

"Yes, my son," said Will, "more dan one too, by God, 'ey?"

"That's for sure." I hung up and found Carol staring at me funny. "What's the matter with you?"

"Nothing."

So I moved away, and she stopped me.

"Andrew, were you in a fight when you were fifteen?"

Anthony was scooping in his twenty-cent win. "Where's Andrew, Will?"

"Yeah, where is old Andrew, Will?" chimed Pat, with a lot of bakery sneakery in his voice.

"Over at his girl's place." said Will.

"Think he knows what to do with her?" says Pat. "Just give me a shot, I'd know what to do wit' her."

Then he gave his dough a couple of good hefty slaps while the other two tried not to laugh. In fact, Anthony tried so hard not to laugh through his mouth that he emptied his nose on his Queens and sevens.

Will was too brave sometimes, in *or* out of the booze. But he had plenty in tonight and Pat knew it.

"You shut your gob, or I'll shut it for ya." he said to Pat,

121

which I thought was pretty good coming from a man who had slipped off the door–frame just a few seconds before.

Pat was smiling. "Oh, listen to that, will ya? What's the matter, my son? Ya don't have the bodyguard wit' ya now, y'know."

Not being one to only go halfway up a ladder, Will waited till things cooled a bit before he started fondling a raspberry pie (not lemon, his favourite, but you can't have everything in that atmosphere). He picked it up, and Pat knew just what to say.

"Now, put that down!"

Which might have been the right thing to say but not the right person to say it to; because now that he had it off the table, Will was committed, and if you know Will, you'll know that he never backtracks.

However, he did go halfway, by throwing a dollar bill into Pat's flour. "Dere. I'll pay for da bloody ting."

"You pay out front, and the front just closed. Put it down."

"Gimme me money first," said the pieman.

"The money's for the beer," said fat Jim Rubie.

"Yeah," smirked Pat, and stuffed the bill into a pocket.

Will glanced at all of them, then grinned at Pat and held out his hand for the money, giving him a chance, maybe the last one, to be friendly.

"Come on Pat—gimme me money!"

"No. Now put down the goddamn pie!"

So far, not bad for a little bake shop drama, is it? Pat Lane, with Will's dollar; Will Cole with Pat's Raspberry pie (now at shoulder level) and two bored card-players, bright-eyed at this possible change of pace and already half out of their chairs.

They stood this way for I don't know how long. Well, certainly until Will's index finger had punctured the bottom of the pie, allowing the red raspberry juice to flow freely down between his fingers, to his elbow, to his jacket pocket, through his jacket pocket, down the outseam of his baggy pants, and onto his boot where it stopped. He didn't dare take the time to lick his fingers. He was relieved when Pat flicked a handful of flour at him, because it meant he could let go of the pie, which he did.

Pat caught it, which was the only thing to do at the time. The pie baptized his freshly ironed white smock with raspberries picked at Rattling Brook.

"Now—see? How'd ya like dat?" said Will, in the stunned and almost comical quiet that followed.

"All right," said Raspberry Pat, "let's throw the bastard out."

That was all Will needed to arm himself with an enormous weighing pan full of flour to threaten Pat, Jim, and Anthony—who suddenly began to look a lot like the Three Masked Bandits of the River Platte to old Tom Mix there. So with a great "TADDERANTADDAH-H-H," he backed up, found an opening and took off around the room. In and out of the aisles, behind the ovens, and, for a finish, he one-handed himself across a flour-sprinkled table top without disturbing a single speck of flour in his weighing pan. His landing wasn't all that lightfooted, but he soon recovered and was now laughing too hard to see that they were backing him into a corner full of trays stacked to the ceiling.

If you didn't know that he'd had an enormous weighing pan full of flour dumped over him, you might have thought that he was just a big firefly out for a walk, as he stepped out of the alley behind the bakeshop and into the vast, pitch-black parking lot where his great, complimentary talent for laughing at himself made him crouch, then leap a terrific distance into the air, and come to earth on both of those bad-looking flat feet—instantly creating a lovely halo of Mr. Moore's flour around himself. For that brief second, he could have been some sort of foolish angel who took the wrong turn.

A last check through the town, to make sure that no one would be up any later than him, brought him down the main street and across the park, where he stopped, had a pee, found a cigarette, accidently snapped it in two while trying to knock the flour off it, lit one piece, and continued on his aimless course. Well, nearly aimless. He found a spot that seemed completely wrapped in stars and stretched out to enjoy them.

It seemed only an instant to Sunday morning, when Will arose from the base of the tree. The remnants of the flour had found their perfect mixing partner in the dew that had built up on him in the last few hours. So, laden down with this extra feature, and with hair that looked as though he could have lifted it right off and carried it in a bag, he lumbered, stiff-legged and stone-like, up the path and on towards his house and a big bowl of Mary's porridge, with lassey all over it, and a big cup of tea.

Mr. and Mrs. Thomas still don't know who that *papier-mâché* figure was that said good morning to them that morning, and neither does Vera Throke, Mr. and Mrs. Milley, Mrs. Snow, or any of the other nice, decent folks on their way to church that day.

Although I don't suppose old Mr. Curtis and his son, Gerald, could be counted. Old Mr. Curtis had been recovering very nicely from a hip operation, and that was his first day out in the sunshine.

"Well, will you look at that? Some sight, he is," said the old fellow as Will came close.

"Yes," said Gerald, "If I'm not mistaken, that's Will Cole."

Will gave them a sharp salute. "Mr. Curtis! Gerald!" and kicked open his gate. Between there and the front steps, it took three dings and two dongs from the church bell to penetrate the flour in his ears and get the message from the head to the feet. But even so, he was dressed all wrong for my wedding, and when Will found it out, the whole town found it out.

"HOLY JUMPIN'! ANDREW'S GETTIN' MARRIED DIS MORNING!" and before old Mr. Curtis could turn his creaky neck, Will was upon him, asking for the time of day.

"AHHH-H-h-hhhhh!" screamed the old man, which wasn't what Will asked for, but it would have to do. "GERALD! GERALD!"

Gerald was a great help. "He's nuts!" was what he said.

124

"WHAT TIME IS IT? WHAT TIME IS IT? GIVE ME THE TIME!" Will screamed like the white rabbit.

"GO 'WAY! GET HIM AWAY FROM ME!" said the old man, holding his new hip together; but Will was off and running down the hills towards the ding-dongs which came nearer with every corner he took.

"I'M BEST-MAN!" could be heard richocheting off the rooftops for the rest of that day.

The double doors were open and some of the guests had already spilled out onto the steps. Then, organized by my brother Cec (Will's last-minute replacement as best-man), they gave us their handfuls of rice, as Carol and me came out. I remember feeling lucky and happy and I was no longer thinking of Frank Downs and his round little gut, as we made our way past her folks and mine and Ruth Lowe and weather-beaten old Williams in his good serge suit, flower and all. (I gave him the flower myself. "Get away from me with that, Scott!" but he took it anyway, and now I could see that it was in his lapel. Not properly pinned on, but it was there.)

We had not yet arrived at the big iron gate when Will came clattering down the sidewalk and, in all his beauty, joined those that were already waiting.

He hung there for quite awhile, heaving from his run down through the town. I got Carol inside the car, shut ourselves off from the outside world, and just got nicely settled when Will sliced his way through to the open window and stuck his head in.

"HEY BUDDY, SOME BEST MAN I AM." Then he almost came the rest of the way in and demanded a kiss from the bride, which he got. And as he removed himself, I gave him the tie I promised to bring for him.

"Will, boy, I think it's time to grow up now." I said. Even as I said it, I was sorry, and for the next half hour I hoped I hadn't sounded cruel.

It seemed as though he never heard me because he kept his flashy grin throughout, and, as the car moved away, he banged it hard with his hand for good luck.

The sidewalk was suddenly empty. He turned and faced Ruth. She was hurt and showed it. Hurt for him, hurt because of him, hurt for Carol and me, hurt for everything, including herself. She showed just how sophisticated she had become lately by her choice of outfit and hairstyle, and there was always that lovely, easy smile for anyone who wanted it. The smile that sustained her through someone else's wedding day; but the smile that she could not and would not spare at this time for the half-human, half-rock town-square statue in front of her.

He was very aware of her feelings at that moment but for all that shot her a last-second grin, swung away from her, and passed old Williams—firing his fingers at the old cop's gut.

"Bang, bang, Williams!"

"Nice goin' Cole."

There were such things as grownups, and now he knew it, and I had become one of them. He could hardly give credit to the fact that they would sooner be that way, than the way *he* was.

"Where are ya goin' for the honeymoon?" Will had asked a few days before.

"One night in the Holiday Inn here in town." I answered.

"Jesus, you're really layin' it on, idden ya?"

But it was good enough. Do you know that that night was my very first night in a hotel, with or without a girl. Oh, I had attempted a little upright job with Clarice Knowles at the back of the hotel once, but never got inside.

And now, here we were. I had a mind to use up everything they had to offer. All the towels, facecloths, TV (morning and night, whether we watched or not), room service, and every drawer in the dresser. I was already in bed. I allowed one brief thought for the wedding ceremony, one brief flicker for Will, and that was it. No more. There were all the wedding presents piled up on the dresser. There was I, in bed, rubbing my hands together (as a matter of fact, it was bloody cold up there, but I figured if I called to ask how to work their heat control, old buddy would get there just when we were making our first baby, so I let it go).

The waiting was kind of good. Not too much though, I thought, as I watched Carol go through her preparations. She must have tried on three or four different outfits in there. Ordinary nightie, flannel nightie, pants and tops, pants and no tops, tops and no pants—and all different. I never saw such a carry-on. I felt underdressed with nothing on atall.

Well, after all the modelling and her second bottle of coke, she came out wearing half the last thing she tried on, and it still had the tag on it. I didn't tell her, but before I could get my hands on her, she was over playing with the gifts.

As badly as I wanted her, I knew it would be wrong to behave like the mad animal I'd raised myself to be, so I hung loose for a while longer and watched. She had a great collection of about thirty thin bracelets on her arm, which she removed one by one and stacked neatly into two piles on the coffee table. She was thinking about seeing how many she could get in one pile, but I coughed and threw her off. She finally got as near to me as the small table at the side of the bed.

"I'm sorry, I'm so nervous, Andrew."

"That's all right. I'll turn out the light. I figure you'll want that."

"Yes, thank you Andrew."

I had my hand all perfectly formed to grab one but I waited till she got in bed, which she did but got right out again because I'd slipped under the wrong sheet. It might have given us a new way of doing it, but certainly not the easiest way that came to mind.

Funny how all that waiting helps the stew, though, isn't it? All of a sudden, you couldn't have kept us down with a lion tamer's whip. Most of it was fumbling for position, but the reward was close enough. And because it was so near and everything else was so simple and natural, we allowed ourselves that last precious pause before contact. We shouldn't have waited.

127

"A-N-D-R-E-W!"

It could have been some other Andrew, but it wasn't. It could have been someone else's voice, but it wasn't.

"Oh, my God," said Carol, and put on everything she'd taken off.

"Sh-h-h . . ." I managed.

Then the voice again: "HEY, ANDREW! WHAT ROOM ARE YA IN, ANDREW?"

"Who is it?" Carol said. A little too loudly, I thought.

"Shut up!" I said, which stunned her a bit.

"Andrew, don't say that to me."

"Sorry. It's Will."

"Oh shit!" (Her little note of truth in a time of stress.)

It was him all right, and as I leaned out the window and spotted him, he spotted me. He was perched upon the pool wall between two lamps and was swinging his legs.

"Hello dere, Andrew." he said.

"Oh, please go 'way. Please." said my new wife. I followed that with a "Bastard."

"Hey Andrew. I left a bottle at da desk for ya. I know yer busy so I'll say goodnight."

With that good news, I slipped back into the room, back into bed, and was getting her back to normal with a gentle, gentle kiss when: "I CAN TELL YA RIGHT NOW, YOU'RE NOT DOIN' IT RIGHT!" came in through our window and into our bed.

One of the biggest insults you can pay a girl is to laugh on her lips—and I did it. Twice.

If Will hadn't been criticizing one of the few things I do very well, he would have heard Williams come barrelling up behind him. When Will swivelled around on the wall and dropped, he almost slid down William's chest and gut.

"That you, doin' the shouting?"

"Dat's me, all right," said Will.

"What's wrong with you? Gone nuts?"

"Yep."

"Who is it, anyway?"

"Andrew."

"Well, that's one taken care of. For tonight, anyway."

128

Will had already started to walk away from him.

"I can't take my eyes off you for a second, can I?" said Williams. "You're more trouble than a school of dogfish. Look here, I'm talking to you!"

"I can still hear ya," said Will, on the move.

Williams kept on. "Leave it to you to spoil a fellow's honeymoon. That's cruel, b'y, cruel. I hope you're bloody well ashamed."

"I am," Will shot back, "It's sometin' shockin' what's goin' on in dat room."

Williams was shouting now. "I DIDN'T MEAN THAT!"

Will turned and looked at him from a great distance. "Is dat you doin' da shoutin'? Dere's people asleep aroun' here y'know."

All Williams could do was shake his fist at Will, and as Will thought about what he was going to do with the rest of the night, Williams was wondering the same thing.

I knew one thing he *did*—go to Henry's Bar-Restaurant. Ordinarily, it would've been just about closing time, but a tableful of ladies were throwing a small birthday dinner. That gave Will a bit longer than he might have had otherwise.

Henry's fat, hairy fingers fumbled for and counted out forty-five small candles that he would use on the pink and white, slightly-caved-in cake on the counter in front of Will, who was yawning a bit into his sixth beer. He had another look at Joyce Love, the birthday lady, and shook his head.

"Get out of it, she's older dan forty-five."

"She's forty-five, so just shut up," said Henry.

"Go 'way wit' ya. Forty-five. Sure she's got a daughter almost dat. Forty-five."

"Just give us a hand getting them lit!" snapped Henry. So the two of them went to work. And when they'd finished, Henry carried the thing to the ladies' table, starting up his "Happy Birthday" before he got there.

When everyone else sang, so did Will from the farthest stool. In fact, his singing became bolder and lustier than anyone else's, and when they finished that one, he swung right into "Jolly Good Fellow," and for some reason rolled into "Pack up your Troubles," "Tipperary," and "Auld Lang Syne," although it wasn't anywhere near New Year's eve.

Will was "the King of the Castle" until he stopped to sip his beer. When that happened, Joyce Love slipped in her speech and the momentum was lost—and so was Will. For a while, he was completely wrapped up in their happiness, but now he was on his own again. He'd been alone plenty of times before, but this was the first time it really got to him and he wasn't too sure how to handle it.

Suddenly there were voices louder than his, and boots that danced faster, and all his "buddies" had other buddies, and he couldn't figure it out.

I figured it out. And knowing Will as I did, I knew that he would be, as always, the last to be awakened by a change of life. Not *the* change, but *one* of an *unlimited* number of changes that were available for the receiving. I was sure, for example, that Carol had brought about one of those changes. And it happened naturally, the way they're supposed to happen.

Then there were those changes that I would have to make happen (and they're fine too), but I liked the others because I'm as lazy as a cut cat. I don't mind being carried away by life. I'll see the dangers in time, if there are any. But in the meantime, wouldn't it be grand for Carol and me to go along for the ride?

I never thought anything special about the human being called Andrew Scott. I was never taken with the way I looked—in my clothes or out of them—and I'm surprised to hell that Carol ever was. I hated to get into the same old workclothes day after day, and then the same old sweater and pants and shoes after I'd come home. I was lazy, but I was also always concerned about never knowing which road to take, and worse than that, not being qualified to take any of them.

Carol taught me better. It wouldn't have mattered to her if I had dropped out of the race, because it wouldn't have mattered to her if I had won.

I have to be careful now or I'll start talking like Will again. He does that to Andrew Scott.

They used to call me his bodyguard and things like that: I was bigger than him, and I wasn't too bad in a fight, and I didn't let him get hit very much, but that's were it ended. Will was often surprised because he left himself wide open. Not only in a scrap but all through life. Then when the surprise came, he would either pay it the attention it required or not, depending on his mood. Either way, it was as if it never happened.

I was, most unhappily, the direct opposite. I used to slow down when I came to the end of a building or a hedge or something, because I figured someone was waiting to surprise me. This happened all the time. I haven't done anything important because I always figured: That person that's been hiding around the corner with the rolled up fist would take it away from me anyway. I don't like surprises, that's all there is to it.

Let's say I'm going to a party. I'll tell you before I go into the house that I'm going to have a bad time. It's easy when you catch onto it. See, that way I'd come away from there not being disappointed or surprised. Those other people who were having a good time for themselves never knew about that fellow behind the door. But they will, now that he's not waiting for me anymore.

See, I finally met him. But not before Carol and me had found a place, got a TV, the promise of a son, and had shovelled one winter's driveway. And while the memories of that first season are fresh, let me put off for just a few minutes more the telling of my ultimate surprise.

I had come up a winner with Carol Tilley, no doubt about that. But although I could gloat over my liberation from the old life, much too long in coming, and my eyes were coming unglued for the first time, I knew that there was at least one adjustment that I'd have trouble getting the hang of: Time.

Will, in his style, couldn't tell time. Or you'd certainly think so. You know when you ask, "Do you know what time it is?" of most people, and they say, "I don't know." They may not, but at least they know it's one hour one way or the other. When Will said it, he meant it. He knew Friday was fishcakes and paycheck. And pea soup and dumplings said it was Saturday. But that, and the quitting whistle at the mill, made up the only calendar he recognized. (He could never get together with the starting whistle.)

I mention it because I became the same as Will, knowing him for my lifetime. And then, like a light coming on in a cold cellar, I was been told that I was thirty-six years old, and, unlike my friend, his disciple had a hard time getting used to it. If only I'd known how young it was—to be thirty-six.

Not yet, not yet. The man around the corner of the woodshed can wait a minute longer.

What else was there to catch up on (because this once I didn't want to be last), to remember (just for remembering), to put in order (so my poor lazy brain could keep account of who I was and what I was about)? Well, my lunchbox had a bronze name-plate on it, telling them who I was. That was one thing I could count on. *Andrew Scott*, it said, plain as anything.

So there *was* an Andrew Scott. I was beginning to wonder. It all seemed so short and one-dimensional.

Not a genius, they can say that, but a fairly decent head on his shoulders, they should give me *that*. Not well travelled. In fact, back and forth to work and to the club and back —just about does it for someone as easy to please as me.

A spud and beef man. Although I would have tried just about anything offered me. Girls? When I was single I looked for the nice ones. They could be plain, as long as they were nice. In fact, they could be from out of the swamp, but they had to be nice. No, Carol, with you, my love, I had it lucky on all sides.

Drink? Well, I suppose we had a taste of everything at one time or another. Home brew, scotch, rye, gin, bourbon, vodka, brandy, all the usuals; and then the unusuals, when we began to get a bit more selective, taking us into the realm of the extracts—vanilla and so on, and on to the exotic lotions: from the kind a man puts on his face, to the kind a woman puts behind her ear. Once or twice we tucked into a dozen or so tall bottles of Cold Pine and Tar, which had just enough alcohol in it to spark one match and was very good for disorders that might have been brought on by bootleg screech or lily of the valley perfume or liquid shoe polish. Yes, it was good for all those three. The polish went well when you weren't getting the most out of your toothpaste, or you didn't want to look a girl in the face for eighteen months or so.

I think the only things Will didn't try were canned heat (which wasn't around when he had formed his drinking tastes) and antifreeze (which he once had about an inch from drinking time, when the old fellow who had handed it to him fell over dead from it).

With all of this, you'd say that Will was a drinking man. Well, now and then he'd get into it all right, but mostly he was a taster. A big taster. Of everything that was handed him, in a glass or bowl or vase; of everything that passed him in the street, or that tempted his muscle or wit, or had teased his tastebuds. In fact, on many an occasion while Will was enjoying the fullness of everything that made up his evenings—the people, the music, the excitement—I would be content to concentrate on the fullness of the beer. And I've been known to end up much worse than he.

When Carol told me she was pregnant, for instance, I couldn't find enough to drink to calm my nerves. But if you don't mind, I won't talk about the baby to come. Boy, girl, or whatever it was going to be. It would distract me too much to talk about it. I wish to hell I weren't so easily distracted. One thing at a time, that's me, and that used to be too much by half.

"Where is he? Have you seen him lately?"

No, not Will—the man behind the corner of the woodshed, my surprise.

"Or has he gone, now that he's got what he came for?"

If so, then I guess it's time to tell.

*   *   *   *   *

It was Monday. It was cold and I was rushing for the punch office, with my high mackinaw collar up over my

133

ears, when Will showed up behind me. Things had been different for awhile. Oh, nothing that unusual, I suppose. It was just that we hadn't seen as much of each other as we used to, which used to be all the time. Will was the same as always, but maybe I was looking for a change in his attitude towards me, the old married man. Happily married man. I wondered if he thought I was happier with Carol than I was with him.

"Marriage agrees wit' ya," he said, "Ya looks fifty-five."

"Hey there, my son, we need a godfather, how d'ya like that?"

A sharp blast of wind attacked us at the corner of the building, so I didn't get his first reaction, but his next one seemed genuine enough.

"I s'pose, now, I got to get a tie," he said in a voice high enough to top the wind.

After we got inside I told him that Carol had been asking about him.

"Yeah, I figured dat," he said. "She hasn't got over me yet."

"Food is the only thing you'll get from her, my son. 'Drag him over after work so he doesn't get time to go home and change his mind like the other twenty five times he's been invited!' she said, so we're doin' that, after work."

"Dat'll be da day. I'll come over when she learns how to cook." he said.

"She knows how to cook."

"Sure—sure—"

"All right, we'll send out for something. We'll pick up some Chinese food on the way home. Or some chicken."

"It'd drive me nuts, b'y. Drive me nuts."

"What would? Old friends?"

He was still smiling, but he couldn't get into his dirty singlet and down to the machine fast enough.

"Da room, b'y. Da room."

"What room? It's a house, for Christ's sake. There are six rooms, if you want to know how many."

"No, dere's not. Dere's *one* room. Dat's da one you start out in; dat's da one you come back to after ya go to the t'ilet, and dat's da one ya finish up in when it's time to go."

I was getting good and bloody mad by now. "SURE. THE LIVING ROOM. THAT'S WHAT YOU'RE TALKING ABOUT?"

"Livin' room? You can't do your *livin'* in a room, old man."

"Sure you can."

"Not me."

"Well, Jesus, you don't have to, you know. I'll feed you on the back steps, or we'll go out or something."

"No b'y. It's all right. What're ya carryin' on about?"

I couldn't believe any of this. "Are you telling me that you're never going to come to my house?"

He shrugged.

"I don't want your frigging shrugs," I shouted. "What's wrong with Carol and me and the house that you won't come up and see us? WHAT?"

He'd already given his answer and I knew he wouldn't give it again, but I kept on. Not long ago I would have been satisfied, but not now.

"THEN SHAG YOU!" I shouted, as he swaggered away. "Don't think you're better than I am brother, because you're not. YOU'RE NOT, WILL!"

But he was already swallowed up in the sound of the machines and their music. That's right! Will claimed that he could hear music in that incredible constant sound. At times whole tunes, from beginning to end. Now and then a popular tune that he only knew a few notes of, but he would get the rest of it from the rolling machines. Mainly the music was classical. That's nuts, hey? True though. And guess where else he heard music? At the cove. When the river water got caught up in the mouth of that cove, it went crazy. Will loved it and would watch it for hours. Sometimes sitting so close that he'd get splashed all over for hours on end.

As usual, the music he heard that day at the mill was known only to him, and even as I passed close by him at the stack on my way to the wet end of No. 8 machine, the words of the song being formed by his wide open mouth

135

were a complete mystery to everyone but Will and his sensitive eardrums.

So, as each enormous, glittering cylinder began to accept it's share of that Monday's first newsprint, I put myself to work at the wet end, much relieved that I wouldn't have to talk to the fool until lunch-time, and maybe not even then. I wouldn't. That's it, then. I'd call Carol instead. The hell with him. You can call it childish or anything you want, but he started it.

Now, why couldn't I have gotten my wish? But no sir. And why did the paper choose to break just after I'd slipped and banged my kneecap on a pipe (filling the air with my carefully selected and silent blasphemy)?

That's what I mean, see? It was that fellow from around the corner of the woodshed again. I gave that man a special extra curse and took my bad knee cap to the dry end, where my friend, totally thoughtless of the routine paper break, was singing "I'll Be Seeing You" until the veins popped out of his neck. He had armed himself with an air hose and had moved in on a cornered scrap of paper, having pre-designed its route and fate and teased it towards the broke hole and down in. That was the point he was at when I arrived.

I tried to get behind the stack where young Barry Rose had already been frantically dealing with the steadily mounting waste paper—rising accordion-like in front of his face and raised-up arms. He quickly cut that batch down to size, as his spidery frame raced up its bulk and clawed and yanked and stomped and forced it down the broke hole. Only to have it replaced by a fresh supply which quickly enveloped the young fellow till all you could see were his grabbing, fighting, angry, hairy hands.

As usual, the hellish, screeching noise that followed the break seemed never-ending. The loose paper strips continued to shoot high in the air between the cylinders like white flames out of a black hell, and it was during this time, with the air filled with loose paper which seemed to have a life of it's own, and a near-human desire to win out, that Will decided to fool around with the boy with the bad knee cap.

He blocked me, is what he did. And slapped my face, pinched my cheeks, mussed my hair, tickled my gut, and even clawed open my fly. And we screamed a lot at each other.

"Will, stop screwin' around. Stop it now!"

"Where ya goin' buddy? Where ya goin'?"

"Will, get the hell out of the way! Come on now."

We had a couple of funny, tricky moments right there, with the floor slippery with paper ends; and the fool busting his gut with his oddly timed gaiety. I could have handled him with no trouble at all if I wasn't trying so hard to save my knee cap. So my awkwardness and inability to defend myself properly encouraged him to even more flamboyant risks upon my usually pleasant nature. Soon he was riding my back and calling me "Scout," but a clever twist of the body on my part brought him to the hard floor. But even the crack on his head was not to have too much effect on his mood.

What was next? It was all so soon in coming that each second's breath and motion needs a time cell of it's very own. As Will rolled off my shoulders, I slipped (managing not to land on my knee), got to my feet, and almost made it to the stack before my friend—but not quite. He had raised his hands to stop my entrance.

I faked a move to his right. He shifted that way. I dove under his left arm. He slipped on some paper, I tripped over his flying foot, shot out a hand for the guardrail at the opening of the broke hole, got it—slipped—then got a real good grip, just as the broke hustler (I don't know if it was Barry or someone else by that time) pulled down another great stack of paper, gripped the rail halfway up along, planted his feet firmly onto the prize catch of paper, and began to force the heavy load downward.

I imagined I was safe, as my left hand came up to join my right. I was totally calm and sure that I was all right, even with the thin layer of paper lying lightly across my eyes.

I heard Will's first "ANDREW" from there, half in the hole and completely covered with paper. I almost had a

137

good laugh at how cleverly I had chosen my hiding place. Better than behind Indian Rock—much better than underneath Mr. Locke's woodshed, or in the ladder house in the back lane off Third Avenue. And peace? Don't be talkin'. How much longer could I have stood Will's racket atall? I was beginning to like this. I didn't think he'd ever find me—

Cyril and Ed might tell him. Nah! They don't like him enough for that. Besides, they're too busy playing grounders. Yes sir, this is all right. I knew it was here. They used to call it the dynamite cave. I never knew it was as deep as this though—That's one, two, three, four, five trees. The catamaran won't hold any more than that—Can I have some Christmas cake? Did you see my report card? Look Will, I got my licence—That's the last time I'll get my brother's truck—Leave him alone! Don't you put a hand on him—Will the rope hold? Hee-hee, look at this. Give us a Tarzan yell, Will. No-o, I can't do it. I'm going back down, my hands are burning. WILL! I got a cramp—A CRAMP. I can't hold on anymore—I'm trying—

Will's last "ANDREW" was a scream that stayed with me till my work boots left the broke hole opening and kicked their way into the waiting pulp below.

MARY COLE

At first I thought it was some drunken fool whose foot was keeping the screen door ajar, and whose body had filled our small front porch—but when I found it was Will, I almost dropped.

"My Lord, Will, what's wrong?" I knew immediately that it wasn't drink and wouldn't have been at ten in the morning, only two hours after he'd gone to work.

He awoke almost as soon as I turned his starchy white face towards me and gave me the look of a frightened puppy. "Good God above, what's wrong?" I asked again.

He got up on all fours, shook his head from side to side in wide swoops, looked to the window, looked to the door, then buried his face in the bucket that I kept for dirty shoes and rubbers, and became very, very sick.

It was something he got at the mill, I thought. Someone had played a trick on him and put something awful in his thermos—the kind of thing that happened from time to time. But he'd have no need for his thermos that early in the morning because he never bothered with breaks.

All the shouting in the world would not make him tell me. He finished retching, wiped dry his running eyes and mouth with a scarf that was hanging from a hook, and after a series of choked off shivers, he *cried*. Openly— straight at me. Cried. Something that I'm sure I had never seen the man do, and maybe not even the boy.

He kept on crying up the stairs and into his room, and stopped when I heard his door snap shut.

I'll scream until he tells me. No. I'll go to the mill. No. Then, what would I do? Nothing, like the senseless thing I was?

My cake was burning. I tended to it. I'll call Doctor Janes. No, what was I thinking of atall. I'll call the good family friend and Will's boss, Joe Fenner.

But Joe was thinking the same thing. I answered it, and recognized his flat voice immediately. Then got myself a chair and heard him tell the story, the dreadful story of what had happened between eight and ten that morning. How he himself hadn't seen it but did have a hand in trying to harness Will's madness when it happened and long after, until Will's escape from the mill.

"For a minute there," said Joe Fenner, "we thought Will was going to slip down the hole right after him. It looked like Will was fooling around, and it happened out of that. I think we know that much," said Joe, because Frank Downs and Barry Rose and two or three others had seen it.

Joe, God bless his silver hair, was concerned that it all be treated properly, and that Will, my darling brother, not be affected in all the wrong ways. Amen, Joe Fenner, and thank you, sir!

But that would be up to Will, I thought. Outside opinion was one thing. Hurtful, especially at the beginning, but his own opinion of himself would break him or mend him. And what could I do? This was certainly not something I could scold him for, was it, now? And my kitchen talents were one thing, but it would take more than a jig's dinner to set this day in order.

Will was never one to concentrate on any one problem for a long time, or be at anyone's or anything's mercy, either. But this was something that took him over completely.

I saw him change from the devilish, but happy and playful terror of Sunday, to a haunted, confused and lonely man on Monday. And how he was to get through the funeral day, I didn't know. Or even if he would go. And by the time it arrived, I was convinced he wouldn't. He hadn't been out of his room since the accident.

I was going, I knew that much. I had the strongest feeling in the world to want to be there, for Will, to show through me his grief at the loss of his great friend Andrew, who had taken with him half of my brother's life—and the will to live the rest.

I was already in my black dress, although I hadn't intended to get breakfast in it. That wasn't the only thing I'd done wrong that week, I thought as I pulled my chair into the table and faced my lone porridge bowl and half-burnt, scraped toast. That was when I heard his door open.

The stairs creaked from his heavy step, and I saw him, white shirt and all, come into the kitchen. Pale? My heavens wasn't he pale. His eyes looked as though he had been to a horrible war and had seen it all.

Would he have porridge? Yes, he would. Would he have tea and toast? Yes, he would have it all. Which made me think he was feeling better, but it was more to build up his strength, I believe, for the hardest part of the day to come.

He ate it, too. All. And wanted more, and ate that while I watched him. What a strange and different person my brother is, I thought, as I looked him over. Not just strange, either, but a stranger almost, I suppose because he wasn't laughing at something and bouncing around. And not even a word, which made him seem to be more like a boarder than family.

What would he have been, this Will? The kind who was sitting at the table this morning, I mean. I lifted the hair up off his forehead to see if it resembled Doctor Janes's. Not really, I suppose. But it didn't look unlike the magistrate's. He might have been that, the way he was acting. He was certainly better looking than the magistrate, if nothing else. He gave me a look, so I smoothed his hair and put my hand back in my lap.

Men who are known for making very great decisions have a chin like that, if I'm not mistaken. And those troubled eyes under those aggrieved eyebrows gave him the look of a very important, special and worldly man.

Well, his decision at that moment was whether to scrape his toast or eat it black, and he was not the slightest bit worldly, unless you counted his world—and I always tried to. But he was special. Even when he frustrated you, terrorized you, disgusted you, you knew he was not like any other, and could have been truly "King of the Castle" if he'd have ten minutes alone with some Queen or other.

He stood up and went up the stairs again. I thought for sure he had changed his mind about going, but he returned. This time wearing a tie. It was while I was trimming his wild hair that I remembered the tie as the one that Andrew had given him at the wedding.

He sat upright and didn't get the tiniest bit fidgety, so I snipped away at the hair at his collar-line; and, although he must have felt uncomfortable in the strange shirt and tie, he didn't say a word about it.

I had finished, and added a hat and gloves to my outfit before Will had even left his chair. I watched as he walked to the front door. He looked drugged and very lost as I held his jacket for him.

"Will?—Will?"

This got him moving, and we left the house and started on our terrible walk down the two hills to the church.

I wish I could have talked to him that day. I never could, you know. A shout or two whenever he came home drunk or if he barged in on me in the bathroom, but that was about all. What could I have said to you, Will? Or taught you? That was another thing. I could never have been his teacher. He needed something or someone, but I didn't have it to give. The rest of our family would be at the funeral but they were pretty much the same. He only had himself, and I'm not so sure he even had that, the way he presented himself at the church gate.

We were almost the first to get there. The few who were there were from Windsor, and I didn't know them. I guess Andrew had. They said nothing as we arrived at the steps and neither did we.

I waited while Will mounted the steps. Wouldn't you know it, halfway up he turned over on his poor ankle and had to steady himself on the dividing rail, which shifted and rattled under his weight and brought him the unwanted attention of the people from Windsor. He opened the door of the church with great respect, as if to apologize for hardly ever having opened it before in his life.

There was no one there, but he couldn't have missed the dark grey coffin at the front and the banks of flowers— among them, my mixed carnations and roses. He closed the door again, mentioned to me in a very soft voice that there

142

was no one there, and came down the steps to join me on the side of the church opposite the crowd from Windsor.

It would have been much better for him if the rest had arrived ahead of us. He could have gone almost unnoticed. But it wasn't to be that easy. In fact it seemed almost planned that they should arrive in one long, steady flow, with us right out in the open like that at the side of the steps.

The Squires, the Ludlows, the Littles, the Greenes had come through the big gate and were already halfway up the walk while poor Will tried to engage me in a disjointed and meaningless conversation. I continued to watch the front gate and searched those all-too-familiar faces for signs of ill feeling towards my brother and me. Well, they wouldn't catch me out, by jeepers.

Will was soaking wet by this time. The footsteps of that Wednesday's mourners got closer and closer, and when Will had talked himself out about nothing at all, he allowed his nerves to be taken over completely by each approaching sound.

Would the parade never end? The Foleys, the Dwyers, the Cashins, the Henrahans, the Jackmans, the Smiths, the Pennys, the Caters were coming our way like small armies in black battle-dress. And finally the car that would be carrying poor Carol Scott and her parents pulled up. I tried to see as much as I possibly could past Will's shoulder without being too obvious about it all.

Carol's young brother stepped forward and opened the back door of the car. Carol stepped out and was joined by Ruth Lowe. That was nice of Ruth.

Where in the Lord's name was our family atall? Oh, there was Hilda—where's Gar? Oh, good. He was coming up behind, talking to Don Smythe and Leah. I wanted Lon to be there too. He was closest to Will in age and, although they were totally unalike, Lon's sensitive nature would lend itself nicely to Will's predicament. There was Tom and his Doreen, that very proud and witty lady; and sure enough, they were followed by Lon and Hope. Oh, and look, there was Douglas, my old sailor friend. Now in the music business (the manufacturing end) and still the family friend.

That was good. They were all here in a bunch and were coming towards Will and me. But Will could say nothing to them, nor did he look at them for very long.

"See, Don," said Leah, "I wanted to bring the umbrella, and you said, 'What for?'"

Don didn't hear, he was too busy waving to a tree.

"I didn't know Carol was pregnant," whispered Doreen. But I'm sure it wasn't loud enough for Will to have heard. Anyway, I'm almost certain he knew about it.

Will turned just as Carol walked by. Ruth looked Will's way, gave him a sort of smile and followed Carol into the church. When everyone entered, we did likewise, and I think it was Tom who closed the heavy doors behind us.

What happened next was not good. Because Curly Power and his family had not yet chosen their seats, Will had slid himself quite naturally about halfway along in the very last pew. So the minute the Powers moved in and Will found himself in the middle, he got very upset and started to shiver and sweat—so much so that I could feel his shaking arm muscles through his jacket and my dress. He tried to control it as best he could by gripping both his knees and concentrating on the prayer book in front of him, but it got much worse and very noticeable. I would have given anything I owned to find a soothing word, but I could only manage to put my arm in his and attempt to steady him a bit.

This, for some reason, only triggered his exit, which might have gone unnoticed, had he not stepped on Curly's foot in his eagerness to get by the entire Power family's knees and out the door.

"Dear Jes—" said Curly, in a voice that stopped just short of bringing down the lovely stained glass windows. All I could do was close my eyes and cry my silent tears for the man who, misery-ridden, pale and weak, had found it all too difficult to take. He'd find another way to say goodbye to Andrew.

*   *   *   *   *

It was not surprising that he left his job at the mill. I had just got a small raise the week before, so we were all

144

right in that department. Actually, Joe Fenner got in touch with me about it all and suggested a formal release would be the best thing for Will. That way, Will could get back to work whenever he wanted to. Such would not have been the case if he quit or had been fired. But quit, fired, or released, it made little difference to Will because he had no intention of even discussing it.

He was half a man. And looked it, and felt it. Aside from his trips to the store for tobacco, or up and down the back-roads of our part of town, he barely made himself noticed. The club was out, and so were the good times, as he knew them. Alf Morrow could mend his fence and it would stay mended. Nish Perry could take the new locks off his doors, and the town could rest.

But so much the worse for the town, I think. A pine tree is not a Christmas tree until it's decorated, and when Will removed himself, I think he removed a good part of the tinsel and light from our town. But that's just my opinion.

In the weeks that followed, he was seen at the waterfall, on the playground at the back of the high school, and up on Scotsman's Hill where he could overlook the town and (more specifically) Andrew's church—from which he was carried, and in which he was wed. And the mill, which was now to Will a brooding, sombre, and smoke-breathing monument—critical, and unforgiving in it's silence.

On one special Friday morning, he seemed to perk up a bit. That was not to say he smiled. He never smiled any more. But he was up and about a bit earlier than usual. (This, of course, meant very little one way or the other, as he averaged about three-and-a-half hours a night. I know, because the hot air register told me so.)

But there he was, with that old tin box that I never dared to open but never ceased to wonder about. For the longest time I thought he must have kept it for snaps of girls. Maybe naked girls, and who knows what else? Don't ask me why I thought that. Perhaps because I did find something once. Could he have been only fifteen? Anyway, it was in his shirt pocket. And when I dropped the shirt in the wash, *this* dropped out of its pocket. You're not going

145

to catch me telling you what it was, so don't try me. It wasn't in it's package; that fell out later—small and square with a picture of an Arab on the front, and that's all I'm going to say.

The tin box had puzzled me, but he was allowed his secrets, and I respected that. It was only luck that I overheard his reading of the letter:

"I know the kind of life you want, Stan—" (who in heaven's name was Stan? Did we know a Stan?) "—I know it suits you. But I'm here—all the while. I have to wait. I have a life too, and in my life, I need you. At the same time, I know you don't need me. Is there much more to discover? Haven't you seen everything yet? Are you going to be a rowdyman all your life? I try not to think of you, Stan, but I love you, still—Florence." (Now, who was Florence? Did we know a Florence?) "P.S. If you remember, you'll come to see me."

Whoever they were, they sure got him up on his feet fast enough. He returned the tin box to his room and left.

According to Edwina Hall's phone call, she had seen Will peering into the bank window. At first she didn't expect him to come in. She knew he didn't have an account, and he had hardly ever stepped inside the bank before. But he did go in, looking and feeling out of place and as though everyone's eyes were upon him. He lowered his gaze and stepped ever so softly up to Edwina's cage.

She had great difficulty in acting normal. His new look of a defeated, chronically humble fellow made it so that she was almost afraid to speak to him.

"Will?"

"Edwina."

"Do you have an account, Will?" He shook his head.

"I don't see Ruth Lowe around. Havin' lunch, is she?"

Edwina said she was almost afraid to answer. "She's left."

"Oh." He was very surprised. "Left? For good, ya mean?"

"She got transferred to Toronto. What did you want her for?" (She didn't want to ask, but she certainly wanted to know.)

"Oh—I didn't—" he said. "No. She was the one—she

146

wanted to see me a little while ago. I don't know why. I haven't had time till now."

It was then that he took in the rest of the bank, avoiding those who he thought might have been looking at him.

"Toronto." he said at last.

"Anything else, Will?"

He pointed: "Who's that, Edwina?"

"Who? Oh, that's Russ Curtis's son."

Will appeared to be absolutely stunned by this news.

"Yer foolin'," Will said. "George? I didn't think he was old enough to work. 'magine."

He stood there, as if frozen, until Edwina asked him if he was all right. "Sure." Then he took on a strange expression and looked sharply around to his right, as though a bee had stung him. You remember when someone at school would cave in your knees from behind? That feeling. He almost had to brace himself up. "Where'd they go? I used to know everyone in here." And he left a sympathetic Edwina to her work and came back home, much less the energetic fellow that had left.

Losing Andrew was most certainly the blow of his life, and nothing could ever touch it for heartbreak. But Ruth, too, had filled a corner (however taken for granted she was) which was emptied now by her leaving; and the already raging confusion it added to made heavier the load on his poor head—so he sought a final peace.

He went to the cove. If it was the more innocent time in his life he wanted and needed, he would surely find it among the familiar and friendly rocks that had never, and would never, change. The crashing, bashing river spoke to Will as it never would to another living soul, and played its music for him. And it heard Will's story and listened well —of his old friend's death, and how he, Will, had accounted to himself for it, and had met himself for the first time in his life; and was surprised and not too pleased with what he saw.

What was not explained to him was that he had discovered what most of us had known about ourselves for all our lives. He alone, in the long ago, had escaped onto his own little patch of cloud, had found the higher ground, and played in wider streets unlike our own. And we would secretly have continued to envy him, but for this dreadful awakening.

But now he was able to see. Now, almost silenced by the past few weeks' events and his new-found knowledge of himself as a man with limited courage, he found himself taking the trail to the floor of the cove and adjoining beach; and once there, stepping ever so lightly, almost tiptoeing, across the coloured pebbles that had known his reckless jumps and strides for thirty-six years.

He finally made it to his familiar blond rock at the cove, where almost immediately the spray was too much for him and he was forced to move out of its reach. There was no doubt that as he sat, hunched and tamed, he had surrendered the boy in himself to the humourless man that these recent events had produced.

"Some cold."

He took about as much of the spray as his sensitive skin would stand, and then got up. He looked up and found the easiest way up the red cliff. But he had his mind made up that he would be inching his way back down before he got to the top.

He stopped long enough, two thirds of the way up, to disturb a bees' nest. There he waited to see what the angry things would do. He hoped one wouldn't bite him, but it did. On the back of his hand. There was a time when he would have dared it to bite. But now was different. It hurt him a lot. When he finally got rid of it, he dug his left hand further into its holding place and scraped his right hand up and down the bedrock until it looked as though he was trying to scrape the bee sting away. The round, yellowish bump with the red center grew and grew the higher he got, in his climb to the top.

He made it, but didn't stand up for the longest time. When he did, he turned slowly on the spot and took in the outline of a small part of the town. From the mill and the falls to Fourth Avenue. Goodyears' barn, along to the pipe-

148

line and railway road, and around to the river in front of and below him.

He remembered the accident, as I suspected he always did around this time of day. I'm certain it was always with him in some measure.

He stretched his neck to take in the river, and moved even closer to the edge by squatting down and sliding his boots sideways. Having sent a slew of "nice, juicy, round stones" over the edge and down into the river, he slowly and cautiously brought his top half to an almost upright position. The sight of the current below made him dig his already dirty fingernails even deeper into the tufts of grass and earth behind his seat. His nerves were in no shape to take any more. He got up and backed up until he lost all sight of the river.

Joe Fenner got to the top of the rock but had gone back down again when he saw Will back off from the edge, because he certainly didn't want to embarrass Will. He only hoped to God he was all right.

"HEY, WILL. THAT YOU UP THERE?"

He waited for ages till he saw Will's troubled eyes peer over the edge at him.

"What da hell do ya want?" Will said.

"Are you all right? That's all I want to know. Your sister told me you were here. All I wanted to talk to you about was—"

"Shut yer mout' an' go home."

Joe figured Will knew he was there about work so he shut up. I think Joe was right, too.

"All right," said Joe, "I'll see you later, perhaps. So long, old man." He waited for Will's "So long," but it never came. He returned to the bottom of the hill and waited for Will to show. He did, and got all the way down to the blond rock before Joe started up towards his home.

I had only been in the house for twenty minutes when Will came up the steps and in. But it was strange, I thought, that he should shut both the outside and the inside door. Something there was no need to do in this weather. The

149

inside door, more solid than the other, was his door, the extra door he had shut on himself, and would not—as painfully, heartbreakingly sad as it was for all of us and for himself in particular—open again till I burned our autumn leaves.

During that time, I talked, shouted, gave up shouting, begged, stopped begging, started again, and tried to help make his nightmares go away.

"Dey'll kill me for what I did. Some night when I'm asleep."

No one else would ever hear this kind of talk from Will.

"No they won't," I said, for the thousandth time.

"Den dey'll put me in jail."

"No Will, if they wanted to, they would have come in and got you."

"Ya don't know nuttin' about it, see."

"I do. My Lord, Will, Joe Fenner is our friend, and you should hear the way he talks up for you."

"I almost choked last night. Look at da way I got sick. I spent all dis week tinkin' about it. Not for a second did it let up."

"Then don't think of it, you foolish man. You've done enough to yourself. All your friends would be your friends again if they saw you—and saw that you wanted friends. You could all talk together—and—enjoy yourselves like before. Like you used to, Will. Talk to them, and they'll listen."

"I haven't got anyting to say to dem, so I don't care if dey listen or not, do I?"

"You really don't care?"

"No. Not a bit. Look here, my dear, nobody can fool me or tease me or make me feel small, because I don't have to see dem. I don't need anyting dey got. Not deir money, or deir clothes, or deir cars. But you know what I got, don't ya? Peace and quiet. If you wouldn't make me angry now an' again, I'd never even get angry. I've forgotten how it is to see someting and want it. Because I got no need for anyting. No need! I've learned to pass da time—and mostly I'm healt'ier than any of dem. Dat's someting, hey? I don't give a good goddamn if I ever talks to a livin' soul agin. I learned to live dis way, an' I'll learn to die dis way—an—an'—it's my way an' no one else's. You can be content enough by yerself. An' if your not—so, what difference? What's yours is good enough for awhile. Till ya get tired of it—tired of dem. Lookin' out at dem every day, every month. Seems slow, but it comes. Dere's nuttin' else that can happen to ya. Ya go a bit more—a few more cups of tea, a bit more bread an' jam, an'—it comes. An' dat's da easy part, ain't it?—Mary— ain't it?"

He had been reading in his usual chair by his usual window, with the yellowing, shapeless lace curtains that I'd intended to change for at least six months, when Ruth Lowe came up in a taxi. It had been a long time, and I wondered what he would do.

Well, the first thing was to slowly bend back a corner of page forty-seven (that he'd been on for a week at least), lay it aside, slide out of his chair, and back up into the centre of the room. It was impossible to read his thoughts, if indeed there were any. He looked as he had looked for these many months. The grin was gone and with it the life in his face.

Over his shoulder, I could see Ruth walking across the road to our gate. She was wearing a smart, yellow and blue coat, which she must have bought in Toronto, because I hadn't seen one like it around town.

Will stood there, not knowing what to do but figuring he should do something. He hated what he was going through, I knew that for sure. He ran his fingers through his hair, took out a cigarette, broke it, put half behind his ear and the other half in his mouth, and, for fear she would come right up to our door and into his house, he opened the door and walked out.

Without knowing it, Ruth had very neatly done the impossible, and my heart jumped at the sight of Will stepping out onto the verandah.

RUTH LOWE

He looked at me, wearily, and lit half a cigarette.

"Hello Will." I had my hand on the gate latch but changed my mind and stayed outside, where I thought I would wait for him to make some kind of move.

A man and woman came along the road and passed on behind me.

"Hello there, Will," said the man, with much surprise in his voice.

"Yes, so it is," said his wife, when the man pointed to the verandah. They moved on, looked back once, and kept going.

Will shaded his eyes, saw who they were, came down the two steps in his own sweet time, reached the walk level, looked straight at me, and came up the walk. He squinted from the light and the slight wind, then stopped. And it appeared as though he might go back to the house, but he started again. This time he plunged his hands deep into his pockets and arrived at the gate. He broke his stare and looked up and down the road, relaxing only slightly. I never heard him say hello.

"You're looking fine, Will," I forced myself to say and should not have, for he looked like another person. Pale, gaunt, extra careless of his appearance, and ten years my senior. But his eyes were what made the real difference. They were much more deep-set than before, as if they had retreated from all human contact. And they were totally empty of humour, which was just not Will.

"I've just come down from Toronto."

He was not the slightest bit interested in where I came from or where I was going.

"I'm getting married, Will." He didn't show me if that meant anything to him or not.

"I guess it's about time, isn't it? I'm sure not a Girl Guide anymore. He came down with me from the mainland. That's why I'm home."

153

When he spoke, it dawned on me how long it had been since I'd even heard his voice. I knew he hadn't been seen around for a very long time. Mary had told me a little on the phone before I left, about how he was back to making his old home brew in the family keg, and about how, whenever he got tired of waiting for it to work off properly, he'd drop in a little methylated spirits to raise it's strength. For all that though (and here she was very explicit), he didn't drink all that much. It was more a matter of his wanting to be completely self-sustaining.

He saw no one, if he could manage it. Now and then, of course, it was impossible to avoid every living soul, especially those on the street who, out of sheer curiosity, would stop outside the fence and do their best to get a good look in at Will. "Some foolish looking, they were," said Mary, "standing there in the white sunlight, as saucy as you please, with their long necks stretching as deep into the front yard as they could, to get a look at Will—that they had by now dreamt the most foolish and terrible stories about. Anyway," she said, "there weren't many like that, thank the Lord. Just a scattered few, and one of the Holland kids, who nicknamed him 'The Phantom.' How foolish are people atall? Sure, if Will hadn't been the holy terror that he'd been once upon a time, they wouldn't see a thing wrong with him now. He doesn't go out, that's true, but my dear, he's perfectly all right—and healthy. He shaves every second day. And read? We don't have enough books for him. That's the truth. He's perfectly fine in every way. But, Ruth—He just doesn't care about living very much."

"Roy is his name."

"Who cares about all dat? Look, why'd ya come down here?"

"Just to see you, that's all. Isn't that all right?"

"Ya sure you're not gettin' tired of what's-his-name already?"

"What?"

With his attitude and his total lack of the old charm, he couldn't have been more unlike Will Cole.

"Go on wit' ya, ya got a good memory."

Which meant, I suppose, that he was referring to that seemingly ancient get-together at the church picnic.

He took one long look around, one last look through me, and left me standing.

"I'm goin' in now," he said, already halfway to the house.

"Can I come in?"

He stopped. "What for?"

"To talk. I wanted to see you. Are you all right? I won't stay long if you don't want me to."

"Well, I don't want ya to. I don't want ya in here, all right?"

"I'm not just anybody. I thought you'd like to see me. We can talk for a few minutes, for heaven's sake, can't we?"

He didn't answer, so I opened the gate and followed him inside.

"Hello, Mary."

"Oh my, hello Ruth." She seemed busy elsewhere, so I didn't keep her. She had aged as well, I thought. Pretty though, and it was good to see her.

I tried to be ready for anything with Will, but it was not always possible. He insulted me a great deal at first. Then, for no other reason but to let off steam, he shifted furniture and was almost *frantic* about it. In fact, he moved every stick of furniture but the chair I was sitting on, which he kept looking at until I stood up. He was at it instantly and had it across the room before I could blink.

"I'm movin' furniture. Dat's what I was doin' before you showed up."

"Can I sit down now?" He didn't answer. "I'm certainly not here to upset you, Will."

I looked at my old friend and hoped he'd respond. I felt awfully sad, and even though I wasn't sure of what to say to him, I was sure I had to fill up the time, or he'd say we had nothing to talk about and tell me to leave. All I wanted to do, really, was cry for this man who loved to laugh. This free, free spirit, rotting away by his own hand and will.

"I won't stay long. They're throwing an engagement party for us this evening and I have to shop. Do you see anyone?

155

Any of your friends, Will?" I must have been bothering him a great deal, which wasn't altogether complimentary to me.

"*Will . . . Will . . .* everytime ya say someting, ya say *WILL.*"

"That's your name," I said.

And then, he came fighting back to my question. "Who cares about dem. Dey mout' off about—about how much work dere is goin an' about how nuttin's changed. EVERY-TING IS, AN' DEY KNOW IT."

"They want to do something for you that's all."

"You don't know anyting about it. They blame me. No matter what else dey say, dat's it." He looked at me as though I were the stupidest thing alive. "Don't ya know what I'm talkin' about? What happened?"

"Oh, Will—Will. Now, there's no way they could." I thought he was going to throttle me for my ignorance.

"DAT'S WHAT I SAID, ISN'T IT?"

"It couldn't have been your fault and everyone knows that. Please Will—don't—"

"Ya were dere, were ya? What were ya, the paper tester or someting?"

He walked around and around the room, working up strength to tell me things that I believe he had planned to tell me all along. He uncorked the bottle within, and told his story with force. How, *of course* it was his fault.

"Havin' some fun, I was—an' I went—" he held up his hands as if to show me in mime what he couldn't tell me in words. "—and Andr—"

He stopped and we realized at the same time that he couldn't say his old friend's name. And probably hadn't said it in a long time.

"—and—Andrew Scott went—I sat on top and watched —an' watched. I was just crawlin' around—when—and—" Here he screamed and screamed again. "ANDREW SCOTT. ANDREW SCOTT—fell into the broke hole and went out of sight—and DIED IN THE BEATERS. I shouted to him—" He turned from me and started to break but held up his hand to make sure I'd think twice about going to him.

"I wanted to say I was sorry to Andrew—but he couldn't hear me. He doesn't know I'm sorry."

I stood there like a fool, trying as hard as I could not to allow his words to do the damage to me that they were capable of doing. I didn't want to make it worse by crying all over him.

Then he was strong again. "I ran away from it. Dey called me but I never came back. No, by Jesus, I never came back."

We had been silent for a long time. I had looked away to see where Mary was, and when I looked back it seemed to me he had transformed himself into yet a different person. His story was out, and a strange but still not perfect ideal calm had taken him over. He stood, took in a deep breath, put his hands in his pockets, and sauntered around the room, having a look at me from time to time. I was beginning to lose whatever bravura I'd come in with, and the edgier I got, the more I thought of Roy.

He finally stopped in front of me, his hands still in his pockets. I looked up at him and then away. When I looked back again, it was because his fingers were touching my hair.

"I haven't seen ya in a long time." he said, in someone else's voice.

"I know."

"Long time."

"I'm going to try and get home more often."

"I haven't got anyone y'know. No girl friend."

"Oh?"

"Ya goin' ta stay da night wit' me now?"

The old Will could have gotten away with anything— clean or dirty. He was one of those special people who had a way of getting it said without offending you. But not now. This was different, and I was torn between frustration, fear and fury at the very sight of the man.

"I'm going now." I said.

"Where? To da party, I suppose?"

"Yes, but I have to go home first and get dressed. I'm

157

trying to be nice to you, Will. Will you call me in the morning? Have you still got my number?"

"Goddamn right, I got yer number."

"Goodbye, Will." But he had my arm.

"You're special, aren't ya?"

"Special—come on, Will."

"Sure, you're special. Don't ya remember? Your old lady told ya. Never mind, I had a few. Dey weren't dressed like you are now, but I had 'em just the same. Dey knew deir job—Dey knew what dey were up to—Anytime, dere dey were."

"Yes, I know."

"You got a lot of friends?"

"Some."

"I'll come wit' ya an' scare the jesus out of your friends, how'd dat be?"

"No Will, you can't."

" I didn't mean in the house. You can leave me tied up outside. I'll snap at dem as dey go by."

I had the door open and didn't want to add to what I'd said, so I went outside. He followed.

"I suppose I should try to get a cab," I said.

"A cab! Forgotten how to walk, livin' in Toronto?"

"We liked to talk to each other, remember Will?"

"What do I want to remember? Nuttin'. Go 'way. Go 'way from me!"

"Oh Will, I'm sorry these things have happened to you."

"I DON'T CARE! GO HOME! STOP LOOKIN' AT ME!"

I was not the girl I used to be. Like Will, I had changed. After being an excellent student at school, a clever girl at the bank, and a good conversationalist, with a better-than-average taste in clothes, I thought I needed updating; so I improved upon it all and passed the old Girl Guide with flying colours.

"Will, you're no more than a distant relative to the boy I went to school with, who walked too fast for me to catch up with. And even when he would make fun of me—or even be rude to me—I couldn't get mad at him because all the while he'd have a twinkle in his eye. Well, the twinkle is not there anymore. And you know what? If he were here now, he wouldn't let you treat me the way you have. 'Call me if you need anything—and be careful.' I hope you can be happy with yourself, since that's the way you seem to want it." And I walked away from him.

"No trouble dere!" he shouted. "JUST DO IT, DAT'S ALL."

I looked forward to the party and seeing Roy. I didn't feel guilty, and I didn't care who knew it. Including Will Cole, new or old.

CAROL SCOTT

You may say, "You're not a very nice person, Carol Scott," but I can't help that. It's how I feel and I don't intend to worry about it.

I don't see Will. Regularly, I mean. Of course I've caught glimpses of him here and there, but we didn't become fast friends—and we couldn't. That's all there is to it, and I'm too busy working and keeping a home to give it any more time or thought than that.

Do I blame him? For what? Andrew's death? What odds, whether it happened one way or the other? He's gone. And that's only one fact. Another is that he left a house that needs paint, and another is a son called Terence. That was my father's name. Andrew wanted more than anything to call him Will, but I couldn't have taken that, I'm afraid. I don't know if I do blame Will, but calling my son by his name, every day of the week would get a bit unbearable, that's all.

So we haven't talked atall—oh, once on the phone, but I wouldn't know his family if I passed them on the street today.

Ruth Lowe and I were meeting from time to time, but we never really became chummy. She's nice enough and all that, but we're certainly not alike. She has too comfortable a home life to have things in common with me. Or she did have, anyway. Some said she had been back but intended to make her new home in Toronto, which is where I'd thought about moving. Bernice, my older sister is up there and has asked me to go up. I don't know. I've thought about it. I don't like this town much anymore.

Given time to think about it, I'd say I had Will Cole to thank for that: not liking the town, not being very happy here. But do you suppose I would be? And who else would I blame?

Will Cole was wrong. Always. In all the things he did and didn't do. And how self-centred of him to have asked

—asked, like hell—*demanded* so much of his friends, knowing full well that he had nothing to give in return. He was a very big taker—especially from Andrew. From his cigarettes to his friendship to his life. Oh—did I? Well, pardon me for breathing, but if I said it, I suppose I must have been thinking it. Andrew didn't do it all by himself, *did* he? No, he did not.

I can't wish the good things in life to a man like that. When I saw him, last weekend I believe it was, tending to Mrs. Howse's garden, I remembered that I'd heard he was out and around. And I had Terence out for a stroll. At first, it could have been anyone. He had a shabby looking jacket on and was hunched over, lining up a row of bedding plants. I finally got a good look at him, when he finished, went up to the door, and collected his pay from Mrs. Howse. He stayed long enough to meet Harold, the second eldest boy, coming through the gate from work, and the two of them sat on the back steps and chatted together.

Harold must really have liked Will, because he seemed genuinely happy to see him. I heard him say he was going to get Will a beer. After he went inside, Will looked as though he was going to leave but changed his mind. For most of their conversation Will seemed as though he wanted to get away. Harold did all the smiling and laughing. Will held back. I guess he's not a very happy person. I don't know, but he sure didn't look it.

I've seen him on only one other occasion. He was in a different garden and seemed to be working hard. He still didn't look any happier, but at least the sun seemed to have gotten to his face and hands, and his neck was a deep, sore-looking red. After he'd been working that prong (as if he would bring up gold), he ripped off his shirt. The rest of him was as white as snow. He stayed that way for the rest of the afternoon. I know, because the place was only down from my house on the other side of the road.

Too close for comfort, as far as I was concerned. And you know what? When he was finished down there, I saw him close the gate and start off down the hill—the proper way to go. But then he stopped, looked back up our street and came our way instead: on the other side of the street, mind you, but still he passed right close by. I had to back off from the window. I don't think he looked in. He might have. If he wanted to have a look, he'd have it, I know that much. He went on, thank God. He wouldn't have had any other reason in the world for going to his home this way, but to see if he could catch a glimpse of us.

That was the extent of it. He never showed up again—but he did phone. Only once. And I made sure it was very brief. I wasn't cruel. I couldn't have been cruel if I tried. I just made sure I didn't sound overly friendly.

"Carol—dat you?" His voice was completely lacking in brightness and sounded older.

"Yes, who am I talking to?"

"Will. You know—Will—Cole."

"Hello."

"Hello—how are ya gettin' on, all right?"

"Yes."

"Dat's great b'y, great. Here's da reason I called. I've been doin' a lot of plantin' 'round town, y'know? Flowers, mainly —an' it really got me goin' 'round our place as well. Anyway, I got a collection of plants down here dat you never saw before in yer life. Dey're practically takin' over the place. I'd like to bring some up and put 'em in for ya if ya like. Dere's all kinds of tings here, an' it won't cost ya a cent, naturally."

"There's only a few feet at the back, Will, and I've already filled it up—with morning glories, peonies—things like that. Thanks anyway." I almost asked how he was, but I caught myself just in time.

"Oh—right. Good enough, den, morning glories hey? Proper ting, too."

After another gap, I was able to break away, but not before he offered to paint the house, which he had noticed was in fairly bad shape. I told him it was taken care of and said goodbye.

I handled it pretty well, I thought. I hadn't given him

any encouragement to reopen old wounds, was just sharp enough, and had probably done his conscience a great favour by getting him off the hook, as they say.

So relieved I was that I poured a drink of last Christmas's port, turned on the TV, and flipped through *Movie Life* and *Photoplay*.

BILL EVANS, CONSTABLE

I'm twenty-eight, and I didn't even look that when I hit socked-in Gander in February, and went on to spend two weeks at my mother's brother's place in White Bay, without my uniform. But I looked a hell of a lot older than that after I'd had it on for a month. I took my posting in my mother's home province very seriously, and didn't think one way or the other about the town of Grand Falls, Newfoundland, until I'd given it a lot of time.

I was not outgoing. Never was. So, small town or not, I knew it would take a while before I'd even allow the people to make an impression on me. But that didn't stop me from making an impression on them. And I think I did that. For a while at least. I was cool. So cool that you'd have thought I'd majored in aloofness at school. I rarely said good morning to anyone and wanted no part in off-duty socializing. That was not what I was there for. You never ran across such a policeman. Manufactured, I was. From the store-bought scowl on my face, to the puff in my chest, and my crisp little walk.

After all, I might be a Newfoundlander once removed, but I was also a city man. Born and bred in Ottawa, to be precise. And if I didn't get across the idea that these folks are favoured by my presence, then what was the use in my being here? Where would be my bargaining power?

So then, it was most important that I remain a mystery to them. Strong and silent. Straight as a ramrod. One of the chosen few in blue! And that image would have been launched much more successfully on my very first day had I not been nursing a hell of a tummy ache from the bottle of my Auntie's "bakeapples" which I'd done away with on my trip from White Bay. That left me with only the "rabbit": two medium-sized bottles that I would have to keep my hands off until I'd familiarized myself with the town a bit. Well—at least, the main street.

Mayor—magistrate—lots of churches—well laid out—

friendly faces—nice. Not Ottawa, but nice. The paper mill —great looking hospital—impressive, newly developed residential areas—old *this,* modern *that*—lots of tradition, but signs of keeping up—contentment—beautiful.

I didn't expect to find much in the criminal files, and I was right. One break-in every five or seven years—one suicide (a transient) in fifteen years—no rape—one peeping Tom (so long ago he probably can't remember what he saw)—some poaching suspects (no convictions)—and that was it.

Now who the hell was Will Cole? His name was down so often I thought he was the arresting officer, but he wasn't. Now and then he'd have "drunk and disorderly" opposite his name, but more often than not, there'd be a blank. And not always did it read Will Cole. This fellow might even be in the old files downstairs.

In the files? He *was* the files. He showed up everywhere. From as far back as '46. At first he was down as William Cole (in a print as classy as Old English), but as time went along, it became Will Cole, W. Cole, Will C., just Will, just Cole, W. C., himself, and finally a very impatient, angry scrawl that could've been anything. A man like that had to be dead and buried, or away for the winter, or—resting somewhere, watching my every move. Choosing his own sweet time for his next up-and-at-'em.

I asked about him and didn't have to go beyond the first man on the street.

"Oh, yes. Will Cole. Him. Still around. Still young, at least enough to cause a stir if he put his mind to it. But he's changed his ways. Ran out of gas and disappeared for the longest time, but appeared again and has been peaceful and law-abiding and all of that. He became an entirely different person to the troublemaker and rowdy he'd once been. According to some people, he had:

> nearly set fire to the town,
> done terrible things in the back of the church,
> done terrible things in the front of the theatre,
> stolen from his own flesh and blood,

nearly killed two men with a pickpole,
almost hanged himself with his belt,
put thirty-odd girls in the family way (getting twenty
    lashes for ten of them),
de-railed the Newfie Bullet,
knocked over a minister and his wife with a catama-
    ran,
got a New York businessman drunk on screech and
    rolled him blind (doing you-know-what to his wife
    and two daughters into the bargain)—

and other things that I don't know are all that accurate, so
I'd better not speak about them."

Later on during that first week, I saw him and thought
about him a lot. He had come around a corner on High
Street, picked up a few things in a store, came out and
retraced his steps. He seemed gentle enough to me, although
his set jaw and his slight downward gaze gave him the look
of a man afraid to be recognized. He moved quickly and
avoided looking into people's faces.

Now, let me tell you. That man didn't resemble the one
who showed up at the station two nights later for our first
meeting. I heard the next day that "the resurrection" of
Will Cole had been expected for a little while, but that he
should choose my first week's anniversary to open up, was
purely coincidental.

"WILLIAMS! COME OUT HERE! WILLIAMS!"

The question, who the hell belonged to that voice, was
answered after I'd sprung from my chair, snapped on my
ready-for-anything attitude, and stomped my way outside,
leaving the double doors to close by themselves. I knew
immediately who it was and a secret shiver ran up and
down inside me. But you wouldn't have been able to tell by
my face. Strong. Almost carelessly defiant. I threw myself
into a register almost as low as his own.

"What the hell do you think you're doing?"

I noticed he was cupping a bottle of something or other.

"Tell dat fat old bastard to come out here!"

167

I pointed a finger, and having done so, realized it didn't seem that strong a gesture somehow.

"Put that away! Don't you take one drink." Now that I'd said it, I wished I'd added a curse or two because I sounded like a schoolteacher. But maybe it wasn't too late.

"Who the hell did you say you wanted?" That was enough for now.

"I want Williams. I don't know you, do I?"

"I know you," I answered authoritatively. "That's good enough. Williams is dead."

I should have realized it even as I began to say it and stopped myself. It was as if someone had crept up behind him, wrapped a loop of wire around his neck, and pulled it tight. He just stood there, looking cold without his overcoat, and fingering his bottle as though he might absorb some friendship from it.

"What? old Williams?" He tried to remember if he'd heard about it. He would've heard, surely. "What do ya mean, he's dead?"

"I can't put it any clearer. He died three weeks ago. You a relative?"

He shouted next, and made me feel that I had been stomping on hallowed ground just by talking about it.

"HIM AND ME WERE FRIENDS!"

"Don't you shout at me!"

"What happened to him?"

"He just died. Too old."

He lifted the bottle. "Too old—go on wit' ya—too old!"

"Now look." there was my white finger again. "I told you to put that away."

I mustn't have shouted loud enough because he brought the bottle slowly and deliberately to his lips and took it all down—what was left of it—but still held the empty bottle.

"DID YOU HEAR ME?" I thought I said that a bit late, which angered me further. His eyes never left me.

"Dey don't make 'em like dey used to."

"What does that mean?" I knew what he meant: what was I being so stupid about?

"Dey don't make 'em like Williams."

168

He walked straight by me and up the steps. There he stopped and changed his whole tone of voice and manner with one very deep breath, and went inside.

"Down you go," I said with some strength, as I nudged him on ahead of me. He stopped and looked back at me for some reason and shook his head all the way to his cell.

It wasn't till next morning that he asked me what my name was, and that was after he'd caught my very neatly hand-printed entry of his name in the charge book. I'd watched him and thought about him at night. The man had a different life to most of the others I'd met. A different idea of life, is more to the point. I had no doubt that he lived in a secret passage—a channel that no one else knew about. Perhaps he stored up his and other people's tragedies, digested them in short order, and rid himself of them in another form. Kindness, perhaps. The great scapegoat plan for the world, I thought, in all my sorrowful naïveté would be to unload your problems into this great laundry chute and have them spewed forth as something else. Something better. Now, there's a recycling for you.

I told him my name was Bill. He fingered my badge.

"217," he said. "Bill 217. Good enough."

By the time he left, the sun had been out for two or three hours and the night's light snowfall had already been turned to slush. He stood out on the steps, hugged himself from the cold, and looked out and around High Street. I watched him from inside the door, and just when I opened the door to the inner office, he opened the outer.

"Hey, Bill? Come out for a second will ya?"

I came out.

"Hey, Bill—Hey, Bill—" He wasn't saying anything.

"What?" I almost shouted.

"Hey, Bill, have ya got da time?"

I checked my mother's going-away present. "Nine o'clock."

He smiled slightly and continued to look at everyone and everything but the person he was speaking to.

"Nine o'clock—" he repeated.

"Why? Where are you going now?"

169

He shrugged. "Lots of places." I left him there but returned after he'd opened the door again.

"Hey Bill, Bill, Bill, Bill, Bill." he shouted, till I thought there'd been a murder on the front walk.

"WHAT?"

"Give me a cigarette."

I gave him one, anticipated his next request, and lit it.

"Lovely, tell your mother," he said, and before he moved, he took another moment to look me up and down and around and around, from my youthful, inexperienced face to my Adam's apple to my squeaky new Sam Brown belt to shiny boots—in a kind of appraisal.

Then he smiled, rolled up his fist, and pulled back his elbow. What now? Surely I'm not going to have to lay him out with my gun butt? Instead, he took my hand and shook it once. Vigorously. A sort of semicommittal towards my person.

He obviously had no set plans, but I had to go in. I was cold.

WILL COLE

No one up here. I t'ought dere would be. Wednesday: half-day in da stores.

Now, where's dat nice flat rock I found da last time? Here! Now, don't tell me I don't have any matches. What am I goin' to do wit'out a match? I s'pose I got to go down an' look for one. Well, I won't. I'll wait till someone goes by.

Someone? Dere's no one. Look at dat, would ya? Not a man, woman or child—or dog. Even when I stand up, I can't see anyone. Not only dat, but listen—I can't hear a car. Not a one. Or footsteps—or faraway laughter—or a door slammin'—or sounds from da mill. You'd tink dey all packed up and left, wit'out tellin' me.

Let's see what it's like on da odder side.

Oh, yes. Dere it is. People an' cars an' everyt'ing. Funny, hey? Now why is dat, I wonder? Can dat happen, d'ya s'pose? That a fella can have his own side of da hill, like dat? Live an' breathe in his own little box, like dat?

Well, I s'pose unless I raise the flap, no one will get in, an' eat off me table, an' read me mind, an' watch me fat gut grow. And dat could go on for one helluva long time. Until, as I say, I raise da flap.

I don't know about dat, though. I could get overrun dat way, with not just friendly people wit' beer an' food an' good wishes who would stay for as long as I wanted, but all kinds of strangers too. Wit' back-handed smilin' and hand-me-down clothes. Da sort who've got deir hats and coats on before I've finished me sentence.

Perhaps I'm wrong, but I don't tink ya'll find Constable Bill 217 actin' dat way. I somehow don't tink he likes gettin' dem overdone handshakes either.

Dere it is again! I'm goin' to lean back, here. Ooh—ahh —goddammit, what is dat? It eider stings or flutters.

Now don't be so foolish. I s'pose you're goin' to start puttin' it down to your heart. My son, ya haven't got da brains ya were born wit'. When ya got it on your mind, it's dere.

171

When ya haven't got it on your mind, it's not dere. So stop tinkin' about it an' don't be so foolish. Ya know what it is,' anyway. Ya drinks yer beer too fast.

You used to tink of odder tings. Dat's right, an' it wasn't dat long ago, eider.

Jesus, now dere's someting in me shoe. What else am I goin' to find wrong wit' me before I get home?

I wonder if Pop ever sat up on dis hill. I wonder if he ever sat on dis rock—where I'm sittin'. He might've. Da rock is too heavy to move around, but it makes a bloody good seat. I'll bet he did sit here an' look around. An' brought a girl up too, no doubt. Maybe me mother.

'Course it would have looked different then. Dere wouldn't have been half dese buildings around, an' dis road down below wouldn't have been paved, for anodder ting.

I wonder what he t'ought about on his off-shifts. Da pay rate? His Oddfellows' meetin' at da club—and deir parade? Us kids—an' how to get us over da rough spots?

Den later on he would prob'ly have come up here to tink about his work in da woodroom at da mill—da dust aggravating da pleurisy dat finally would take him out of da mill and put him into—what? Wit' a family of six. What?

Shoe cobblin' was what. He could certainly handle it too. I don't know where da hell he picked it up, but he managed. My God, can't you smell da leather? I'm almost afraid to turn me head for fear he's sittin' right here beside me.

Well, if he does show up, he'll take off again at the sight of me, dat's for certain.

I'm not da laughin' youngster ya last saw, Fodder dear. Gone, he is, an' dere's doubt in me mind dat da young fella ever was here:

> Play me da happy songs,
> Sing me da joyful songs,
> Walk wit' me, dance wit' me, drink wit' me, too.
> Climb da far hill wit' me,
> Lay yerself low wit' me,
> Tell me ya love me, an' ever be true.

172

I should go out to Hilda's and get her to play dat on da organ for me.

Dere's da mill whistle.

Why does it always get cold up here at four o'clock? I need a shot of someting. Rum. For da chill. One long, ten-or fifteen-minute drink, dat'll run right on through and make da flowers grow.

Don't s'pose dere's any sense of droppin' down to da club. It's not dat I don't have da money. I got almost fifteen dollars. It's just dat I'm pretty certain dat dey wouldn't let me in. Da hell wit' dem. If I still feel like rum when I leaves here, I'll pick up a bottle an' go home.

Dere's dat smell of leather again. Some good, dat is. Tinkin' about tings is still a helluva lot better dan doin' tings. Yes, you can say dat again.

Did Pop have any favourite songs, I wonder? Did he ever laugh? Did he walk like me, or who? Did he ever feel young or did he get old too soon?

No, ya wouldn't know me now, skipper. But did ya ever hear me shout, or see me dance, or hear me sing? And didn't you hear me laugh when your old town was asleep? Sure, dat was me. Dat's what I did for a livin'. I did dat. No one else. An' wasn't I loud?, an' couldn't I stir things up, an' wasn't I proud, an' wasn't I foolish—

No. He never saw, an' didn't know about it. He knew me 'way back though. He was around when we built our icy forts to defend ourselves from da snowballs. An' he'd remember me bloody rickets, all right. When da "Goods" (our side) were driven home to tea by da "Bads," makin' me "General" in deir retreat, I was left to protect da fort from me ricket position. An' I can feel dem snowballs now. When dey come over da top and fired all dey had left and more besides at da "general"—now scrunched up in a ball like a baby seal.

Only I can't remember much else. Just glimpses, like old snapshots. Pop at his workbench with his leather, an' last, an' awl, an' curved leather knife with da yellow handle. Pop at da fence, smokin' a cigar dat one of his buddies gave him.

(He didn't look da same wit'out his pipe.) Pop in his derby. Pop wit' his big mug of beer. His moustache, his shavin' strop, his collar studs. His dark and sombre suit and his colourful purple-and-yellow satin sash from da Oddfellows' lodge.

But gone now, and has been for a long, long time. Voiceless, and gone almost long enough to be faceless. Not quite, though.

Now, what tree was it I looked at yesterday? Dere it is, I tink. Dat's da one, all right. Da old one. Now, where's da face dat was in it? Around da side, perhaps. No, I remember I didn't move from dis rock, an' I saw it. Oh, dere it is. What's da matter wit' ya, my son? Are ya blind. It didn't really look like Pop until I'd been concentratin' on it for a good part of an hour, but it's not takin' long today. Da curve in da head at da back, da high forehead, da broken nose dat he got from da recoil on a twelve-guage—No moustache, but it could be him as a young man, like me. Me? Some young I am, dere's no mistake.

My eyes are burnin' again, from looking at it—

"Jesus, Cliff, what a fright!"

"What's the matter with you? Nervous, aren't you Will?"

"Where'd ya come from?"

"From the fire. Move over now an' give us a bit of room. Not bad, is it?"

"What? what?"

"My fire. The shack over there by the field. Right in front of you, for God's sake. You blind, or what?"

"So it is. Didn't see it. What time is it Cliff? (I don't want him aroun'. I'm either goin' to be able to sit here in da quiet, or I'm goin' home.)

"Six o'clock. Getting dark, see."

"Yeah."

"That's about the end of it. Just a bit of smoke left. Well, the hell with that. After all of that."

"Yeah."

"Them and their bloody hoses. There it goes. No. Still a bit over there."

174

"Where?"

"No, it's gone. Hardly enough to keep a fellow warm. I was hoping I'd make it last till morning. 'Tis getting some cold these last few nights. I shouldn't have lit it till midnight. I got no sense of time. See, b'y?"

"If dey'd caught ya, dey'd 'ave put you away for da winter. Den ya'd 'ave been all right."

"No. They did that last winter. This winter they'd probably hang me. Hey, I'd give you a drink but I don't have one."

(I wonder if he'd go 'way somewhere if I gave him a dollar.) "Here's a dollar. How's dat, all right?"

"All right? Yes, my son, I suppose it is all right. It's still someone else's money, though."

(Now, what da hell is he goin' on about?)

"All the time living on someone else's money. Is there anything wrong with that, do you suppose?"

(Dere'd be nuttin' atall wrong wit' it if he'd take it off an' spend it somewhere.)

"Hey, Will. Look at everything changing. I don't like the changes. I'm not ready for them. Jesus, only a little while ago, we were all right, weren't we? There'd be a good keg of beer, a tune or two on the accordion. Wouldn't matter if you couldn't sing. Telling jokes and—and stories and people looking at you when they talked to you. Not half-assed, like now. I left the wife, you know. We haven't seen or heard from each other for years, now. Don't know if you knew that or not, Will."

"Yes. I did. Yes." (Shut up! Shut up!)

"Yes. One night after supper, I was trying to tell her something over the racket on the TV. She'd nod a bit and throw me the odd word, but she didn't so much as look at me for the whole evening. Not a glimmer! And I thought, no sir, goddammit, if she likes listening and looking at the Ned Sullivan show sooner than me, there's bound to be something wrong. So she can have him, I said. And—and his house too, for that matter. I mean, Ned Sullivan was the stranger in my house. You'd think that he'd come second. No, sir. He didn't. He was first. I was the stranger.

175

Well, with me out of the house, and the others grown up and out, she should get a lot of quiet—and be happy. I hope so, Will. Will? Let's you and me put another bill with this one, and go off and find a good sing-song."

"You sing 'em."

"Don't go yet, Will. Sit down here. Sit down. Will, you remember young Joyce. She was the last one. Got married a month ago. They're all gone, now. The five of them. I should be right back where I started, shouldn't I? But, I'm not. You want to hear some terrible news? Heart disease."

"What?" (Shut up for God's sake, shut up!)

"Yes, b'y. Heart disease. I never knew the heart had a disease. The heart stopped, that's all I knew—and you went out like a light, you might say. Jesus, you'd think that people our age wouldn't have to worry about something like that, wouldn't you? Don't go, Will. Not yet. Sit. Sit. There's got to be someone to listen."

"No. Tink I'm goin' ta sit here wit you breathin' all over me, an' goin' on about all of dat? 'People our age.' What da hell are ya talkin' about, buddy? You're sixty, for God's sake. SIXTY."

"Yes, well, how old are you? How old? How old?"

"T'irty-seven."

"Go on with you. *thirty-seven?*"

"T'IRTY-SEVEN, YOU SONOFABITCH."

"Well, might I say, you look older."

(I'd better calm down. Come on now. Watch yerself.) "I'm goin' now."

"Yes b'y. Well, you go then, and God bless you for the dollar bill. We'll have a good sing-song by and by. But don't wait too long Will. Did you hear me, Will?—WILL?"

My God, is dere not enough room in da world for me to have a corner to meself? Where did all of dis come from? I'm a stranger.

Be careful now, gettin' down off da hill. Be quiet, too. Keep an eye out for shadows—an' an ear open for car horns and bicycle bells. Stay out of da darkness—stay out of da light. Watch out for yer friends an' deir families. Don't watch da clock. Keep off ladders and away from stray dogs an' cats. Don't sit in draughts. Don't run—don't walk!

I s'pose dat hill is another place I can't go an' sit. *He'll* show up, sure as hell.

Oh, God. Is dat Walt Little an' his wife comin' up dis way. Dat's not dem, is it? Yes, by God, it is! I'll slip down Bank Road. I'm tired of all of dis.

Look, stop talkin' to me, all of ya! Just leave me alone. No one said dere was a matinee today, leave me alone. Stop listenin' to me, too. I've just been listenin' to meself an' da hell wit' dat. I've never heard meself before. Word for word. I'm someting, ain't I? I don't have an idea in da world. An' now dat I'm aware of it, I prob'ly never did. But everyone just let me go on an' stand right out in front.

Well, how was I? Did I look good? I must have shamed someone—or took someone's life—or shoved a broken bottle into someone's face. Did I? It sounds like I did. What kind of gun did I carry in me belt? How big a rock did I throw?

"Hey, Will! Will?"

"Oh—Tom."

"You went right on by."

"Forgot where I was for a minute. Tinkin' 'bout someting, b'y."

"Is that Will?"

"Yes."

"He was going to go on by and not come in."

"I was tinkin' see, Doreen, an'—"

"We're just sitting down, if you want to stay. Bring him in, Tom."

"Yes, b'y. Come on in."

"She's got enough to feed, wit'out me. I'll go on home."

"Look, I'm freezing out here."

"All—all right." (More of it. Now it'll be late before I get home.) "Nice place, Tom."

"You've been here."

"Never have."

"That's right, Tom. We were in the old place down on

177

West Street when Will used to drop by, and that was only once every six months, even then."

"Where is everyone?"

"Everywhere. Some in bed, some out. They'll be home."

"I can't stay very long, y'know."

"We know that. There you are. Start in. Those ribs have more meat on them than you have on yours, I'll tell you. Are you on a fast, or something? Look at the gut on your big brother there."

"Got everything you want, Will?"

"Yes."

"If you're not going to eat it, I'll get it tomorrow."

"Have ya got a—"

"A what?"

"Oh, I know what he wants. Tom, what's the matter with you atall? Get him a drink of something. He hardly had time to relax when I shoved the dinner in front of his face."

"What've we got, Hon? Rum all right, Will?"

"Sure."

"Here you are. Bottoms up."

"Don't tell him how to drink it."

"He did it anyway. Have some more, Will."

"No, tanks."

"Don't be shy, b'y."

"One is all I need. WHAT'S DAT?"

"Just the door, Will. It's the crowd—no, it's just Susan. Susan, look who's here. Sit down, Will."

"Oh, hiya, Uncle Will."

"Hello dere."

"Wasn't sure who you were at first."

(Wasn't sure who I was. Who would I be but me? Have I got a bag over me head, or what? Now, who da hell is comin' in?)

"Allan, look who's here. Sit down, Will."

"That's not you, is it, Uncle Will?"

"Allan, be quiet. Sure it's Will."

(Well, I wasn't sure which one he was eider.)

"Sit, Will. Eat something more."

178

"No. Got to go now."

"You only had one rib."

"Give the rest to Fannie an' Freddie dere. So long."

Listen to dat. They're laughin'. Is it at what I said? I
haven't heard Tom laugh since—I'm not sure I *ever* heard
him laugh—out loud. Dat's odd as hell, hey?

What's dis? Old Stan's medal. What's dat doin' in me
pocket. I must have dropped it in dere by mistake when
I had da tin box out last.

"Where ya off to, Mary?"

"Royal Stores. Do you need anything?"

"No."

"Are you all right?"

"Yes, girl. I'm all right. All right?"

"Tom just called. Said you had supper there."

"I guess so."

"I'll be back in a little while."

Dere's your medal back, Stan. What d'ya say we take a
run down town an' bring back a couple of live ones. Nice
an' juicy ones. Florence won't mind. Will ya Flo?

"—We wrote to each other when I was in me twenties—
or thirties. I can't remember. She was a brown-haired girl
from Placentia bay. They're sweet letters, Will—"

Yes b'y. Yes. So they are.

"Root, me old sweetheart, how da hell are ya gettin' on?
What? Oh, well—Is Root dere, Mrs. Lowe? Can I speak to
her, please? I'll hang on here. (Holy jumpin'.) ROOT. DIS
IS WILL."

"I thought so. Are you all right? I called."

"I'm number one—oh, came across a few friends, y'know.
I'm not takin' you away from your supper, am I?"

"No, no. I'm glad I finally got you. We're off tomorrow,
and I was in a panic that I wouldn't be able to find you
before—"

"Yer off? For where? What d'ya mean, yer off?"

"Well, we've got to be going back to Toronto. Will—I
told you, remember?"

"Nah, we're goin' to get 'er goin' again, hey, my old sweetheart? So you can't go away for a spell. You stay here."

"Will—I have to. My home is there now. That's where Roy's work is."

"Who?"

"Roy—"

"Who? Well Jesus, now ya could've told me."

"I did, Will, remember?"

"Never mind dat. Look, come out wit' me, now. I'll meet ya somewhere if ya like. An' ya don't have to ask anyone. Just come, dat's all. Just say I said so. WHAT? Hey, Root? Hey, what about da times we had, hey? Funny how all da good times stick in yer head isn't it. I'll never forget da great times at school—hey? You an' me an' old Andrew, hey? Den—berry pickin'—dances—PICNIC."

"Oh, Will—well—I guess so."

"Sure, we did have fun together. We did. Ya just don't remember, dat's all. Know what? Now, don't hang up now, when I tell ya dis—but, I always had it for ya, y'know. I just didn't talk about it too much, dat's all. Dere was no one as good lookin' as you in da whole school. Never mind in da school, in da whole town. But, you know—somehow, I could hardly get ya to look at me, half da time. I kept tryin' an tryin'—"

"Will—um—look. I'll be back sometime in the fall, and we'll get together then, OK?"

"I CAN'T FIND ANYONE! You stay—an' let's go an' dig up da good times again. I'm goin' to come up wit' a good job next week. Dey're payin' about a hundred an' sixty dollars a week now. An' dey got a new machine an' we'll have—"

"Will, look. Please make it easier for me. Try to understand. You want to do something for me. You'll get the job. Then."

"Den we'll do it."

"I'm going back tomorrow. You get the job. Get settled and when September comes—Goodbye Will."

"All right, my old sweetheart. SO LONG, NOW!"

Well. Well, dat's over. Goin' to have a drink of beer, now.

* * * * *

How're all of ya gettin' on anyway, all right? Good enough. Got anyting you want to ask me? Or anyting you want to talk about? You're sure, now? Now's your chance to talk to da man himself. Come on, how often are we goin' to run across each other? Anyting atall. All right, den.

Do ya figure dis is about it for me, then? Can I wrap meself up an' add me to the trunk? All right, you tell me when. I'd certainly hate to have to tell stories on meself. I might make a mistake along da way.

Well, let's go for a short walk. Ya don't want to go for a walk? Why? Tired out? If dat's da reason, all right. I knew it wouldn't be because ya didn't want to walk wit' me. Everyone knows I'm perfectly fit to be seen wit'.

First of all, I'm prob'ly the likeliest bachelor around. A bit gamey, mind you. Short on breath, tall on tales; not by a hundred miles a purified man; not as trusting or trustworthy as yer priest, or as faithful as yer dog; I don't stay around as long as yer common cold, but I'm not as brief as yer milkman, eider.

Shall we talk about laughter? Do you get tired of laughin'. I'm the fella who laughed at me sister Leah's mumps, an' at me brother Tom's attack of St. Vitus Dance. An' I almost needed surgery when an old and staid aunt of mine from Nipper's Harbour brought her Victorian background to our lace-covered Sunday table and farted her way through "Fibber McGee an' Molly."

Dat was natural, everyone said at the time. Sure it was. An' so was Mag Sellars droppin' her ninth baby girl comin' down a circus slide. Natural. Clean as a whistle, dat was, an' no mistake. I mean if we're goin' to tell stories about people, stand back. It's a grand day for it.

No. I can't be boddered.

Now, who's dat, comin' down da steps of da store across da street? You know who dat looks like? A—a—she's been away for a long time—a—where's me coat?

Now, I'll wait till she gets closer. *Goodman.* Goodman—
Phyllis Goodman, dat's who it is. Didn't tink I was goin' to
know her, did ya?

"Hello, Will."

"Wha?"

"Will. You'd better say hello to me, by the holy—"

"Hello, Phyllis."

"You don't look so good."

"I know I don't. I'm surprised ya knew me."

"Well, I've only been gone two years. Think I'd forget old
faces? Especially your old face."

"I figured it was about two years."

"You're quiet. Are you sick or something, Will?"

"How've *you* been?"

"Wonderful. In the pink. In the black, too. We got a small
dress shop in Montreal, me and my husband."

"Got married?"

"Yeah. You?"

"No, not me."

"No, who'd have you, you awful thing. You were terrible,
you were. I shouldn't have been caught in a corner with
you. No, it was my mother's pantry. Worse!"

"Oh, yeah."

"My husband's name is LaVallee. I'm Phyllis LaVallee
now."

"Oh, yeah? French, is he?"

"No. German. Certainly he's French. LaVallee. French."

"Yes, dat's what I t'ought. Is he wit' ya now?"

"No, I'm all alone. See?"

"You know what I mean."

"He's in Montreal. Why? What did you ask for? Oh-h-h,
look at that You got pantry on your mind again."

"You know—a—"

"Know what?"

"Nuttin'. So long."

"Just as well, I'm leaving tomorrow morning, early."

"A"

"What's the matter with you, Will?"

"Nuttin', I said."

"You going to tell me? Please, Will. Are you unhappy?
Are you sick?"

"NO. WILL YA SHUT UP ABOUT IT. *Unhappy! Sick!*"

"Can't I ask?"

"A—Phyllis—look—"

"You can tell *me*. Old Phyllis Goodman, who used to act
up with you at recess."

"A—"

"Something?"

"Yeah. I have to—know someting—"

"Mineral? No, animal, I'll bet. What?"

"Would you do—it—again—wit' me?"

"I can't. I'm leaving too soon in the morning, and I'm
busy from now till then."

"But WOULD ya? WOULD YA?"

"If I wasn't going? I don't understand. If we had time,
you mean?"

(What childishness am I goin' on wit' now? No one does
dis. No one is dis stunned. Look at dis, I can't even look at
'er. Old Phyllis Goodman, for God's sake—an' Will Cole—
an' I'm askin' her dat kind of ting. I wish I didn't need to
know.)

"Well, certainly I would. What're you talking about?"

"Wha'?"

"Yes, Will, yes. Is that all you wanted to know? But
you're rotten, making me say a thing like that. Anyway, I
would."

"You would wit' anybody, I s'pose, would ya?"

"Coming around again, you mean? No sir, not anybody."

"Then why da hell would you do it wit' me. WHY?"

"You're Will Cole."

(For a girl who did all her learnin' after school, she certainly had a way with words.)

"An' yer off tomorrow, for sure."

"That's right. And I know you want me to rush out of
town, but don't worry about me, Will, my dear."

"Give us a kiss, Phyl."

"Certainly, sir."

It's late in da day. Me mind's been wanderin' now for at least two hours. I don't feel drunk, and yet I've had my fill. I've got a lot of questions to ask meself, and I can't tink of dem all, but da pressure is dere and won't go away till I've made meself tink.

If da big, wide High Street is empty, I'll walk along it. It should be empty. Accordin' to da Royal Stores clock, it's close to two. See dat empty lot over dere by the post office? Wouldn't I be someting worth havin' around, if I would level that off, clean it up, and have it full of flowers by da time everyone got up in a few hours. Every kind of plant in da world.

Can't do it though. What else? It would take too long to be mayor. I could save a small child from a ragin' fire, or pull someone out of an abandoned mine shaft. Or build anodder, bigger and better "House of God," but I could use dat material to patch roofs.

A bridge across the river! Now, we're gettin' somewhere. And every Sunday we could pack up our little groups and traipse across dis real, nice bridge to—to what? We need a town over dere. Bigger an' better, an' cleaner an' shinier. Da bridge would not have any nameplate, an' da town would not have a statue, because I'm too shy. But we all know a hero when we see one, an' wouldn't I be an improvement over dis present shell.

Maybe I should close my eyes and rub a magic lamp, or pee on a mailbox (whichever I get da chance to do first), and wake up as someone else.

Imagine, Mary! How'd you like to be livin' in da same house wit' the world's greatest dis or dat? Bringin' in more dan you could spend, more dan da Royal Bank could handle. And me in a suit of clothes for a change, and black silk socks up to da knee, and clean nails.

But da great times would happen for ya after I'm dead. "Dis was da house where he was born," you could say. "Dis was his room an' his bed." "Dis is da toilet where he worked out his greatest ideas."

And you, Mary, would have da gentle man you've always
184

wanted around da place—and you'd rather dat, I know you would.

And maybe Root would still be hangin' around. Partakin' of my new and perfect ways. She sure spent enough time and t'ought on da odder one. If I'd had her on salary all dese years, she'd be a grand person for me to know now.

There'd be da two of us. Eaton's catalogue come alive. "She can't be wit' Will Cole," they'd say, "because she's comin' out of da house first, an' dat fella's openin' up da car door for her. What is he, nuts or hypnotized? Oh, he almost caught da tail of her gown in da car door. You nearly got it in da chops dat time, old man. I'd be a little bit more careful if I was you, or you won't get your little bit of you-know-what dis month. He's wearin' a ring, too. Dat's bad. Dat's only a broad jump away from earrings, dat is."

I'd like to help ya Will, my son, but someone like me wouldn't know someone like you. Besides, you'd have an unlisted number, prob'ly.

Root looked nice though. Mind ya, she always did. It's him dat sprung a leak.

Is dat what you wanted, Andrew, my son? Well, why didn't you go an' get it, years ago? You shouldn't have played around so much. What's dat? What're ya talking about? It was me dat played around? My son, dat's some- ting dat I got to get cleared up here. About how Will Cole acted da fool, wasted his life, played around. I knows of fellas who puts on red and blue and yellow and green cos- tumes and spends deir lives runnin' around a rink; an' odder grownups who take deir little bats an' spend deir life tryin' to hit da little ball; an' men who get paid money for hurtin' each other in da ring. I never played wit' life. What I did or didn't do, I took very seriously. If anyone played wit' life, it was you, Andrew b'y. Because you couldn't make up yer mind which way ya wanted to go for a good part of da time. Someone like Carol had to come along and show ya. If dat was what ya wanted from me, I couldn't've done it. But good for her. Good for young Carol.

Anyway, I'm only goin' to say nice things about ya, old

man, because I got a look at the muscles on yer young fella Terence da odder day. (Dere's a name, dere's no mistake.) And Terence might come lookin' for me someday. Dat's if he's not busy on da violin.

Anyway, wit' all dat's gone before an' all dat's comin' after, I'd like to sit an' cry, my son. But I can't allow meself to do it. I'm not a "was" kinda person, nor for dat matter a "goin'-to-be" type. I'm an "am" an' dat's da trouble wit' bein' an "am."

"Hey!"
"What? Where da hell did you come from?"
"Try the sidewalk, or I'm liable to run on over you."
"Well, da truck is big enough all right, but I was here before you, see b'y, dat's da trouble."
"OUT OF THE WAY!"
"WHAT'S DAT?"
"GET OUT OF THE WAY!"
"If you don't quit followin' me, I'm goin' to kick this jeezly ting right out from underneath ya."
"If I had the time, I'd give you the chance."
"Sure ya would. We all knows how tough ya are."
(Gimme a rock before he turns da corner.)
Oh, dere's music comin' outa da mill tonight. Listen! It's not all dere though. No. 6 machine must be down.

How long have I been walkin' atall? Dere's me answer. Da eight o'clock whistle. Will I go home, now? No—not yet.

Dere's one dat says:

COLE

Brian

Beloved son of Bethel and James

17 years

He's not far from Pop's but he's not related. I don't tink so, anyway.

Dere he is:

SCOTT

Andrew

Beloved husband and father

1935-1969

It's cold enough up here, I know dat much.

Well, well, sir:

WILLIAMS

Francis

(Constable)

1901-1971

Your dutiful servant.

Francis? Was dat yer name? I wish I'd known dat. Now, is dis da path I came in by? Yes dis is it all right.

An' da odder one had to go an' get engaged. Didn't ask me. An' I never even put up a fight just walked away an' let 'er go to it. I'm gettin' goddamn tired of bein' last on the list. Dey talk about me, no doubt. "I DON'T LIKE HIM!"

He's not good enough an' I'm goin' to tell 'er, too. What time is it? He's goin' to get a bloody good punch in da chops.

Now, den—I don't have to take Botwood Road all da way. I'll give it da run down the far bank, swish across da top of Circular Road, dart up First an' on to Bank Road, roar up to Beaumont, wheel aroun' an' over to Riverview—

What da hell am I talkin' about? I'll stay on Botwood till I can whip down Monchy, slip down t'rough old man Dormody's place, an' come out on—

Oh shut your mout' an' get on wit' it!

Roy—I'll give 'er Roy! I wonder how she'll like kissin' him wit' no teet' up front. I should leave 'er to him, but the hell wit' dat. A feller gets tired walkin' in horseshit while everyone else walks around it. All right, I'm not what she wants, but if what she wants is some milk-faced arsehole from Toronto, da girl has got to be squared away. He's from da mainland, of course, so he's two planks short of a load, just for dat. I don't give a damn where he's from, he's not gettin' off dis island wit'out a souvenir, dat's for bloody sure. Imagine, though, her an' him!

'Course, she's anodder one. She'll end up meetin' da boats, she will, if I know women. Too bad—too bad.

Roy—Roy. Far as I'm concerned, dere's one too many Roys around. Well, dere's goin' to be one less. Yes, by God, I'm goin' to start cuttin' down on da Roys.

It's a good ting—da next—hill is down—

I was almos' sure—da next hill—was down—Shoulda took da Junction—dis climb is a bitch—What's makin' dat noise? Oh, it's me. Hold on now, hold on—right here. Just get a bit of a rest here—an' get me bearings—

Feelin' not bad, though—little wheezy—Ankle swelling up a bit—odder dan dat—first class. I'll give 'er—Roy—

"Good morning."

"Wha—oh, hello dere—old man—how are ya—gettin' on?"

"Good, good. Anything I can do for you'?'

"You wouldn't have a glass of water, would ya?"

"Yes, sir. I can get that for you. Don't run off now."

Good ting he said dat. Well now, I'll have a nice—glass of—water—catch me breat'—an' go over an'—kill—dat—fella—

I'd be all right—if I could get me knees to go in da same direction—oh, I'm really goin' now. He'll—never—expect it—dis early in da mornin'. One good slug should just about—do it, I'd say. I hope—anyway. 'Cause I don't—want to be up for—manslaughter—or anyting like dat. Dat's it, den—one or two in da face an' across da back—No, no, got to weaken him. I s'pose da kidneys would be wrong, because—dey might never be able to have kids—so, I'll go straight for da kidneys—an' finish him off wit' a "Railway Road uppercut."

Now, den b'ys, here's da street—O-ohh, got a stitch in

me left side—an' dere's da house—Get out da teapot Mudder Lowe—you've got a guest. What's dat—Taxi—Dey was just gettin' ready to leave—Good ting I'm the early bird— Is dat him? Dat thin fella—or is dat da driver? No by God, dat's him, all right—He's slight, sure—Tall though—Never mind, I'll bring him down a floor or two—Hold on dere— He's puttin' da bags in da car. Hold on now—HOLD ON NOW!

"ALL RIGHT NOW—YA BUGGER—I GOT YA!"

"What was that?"

"Oh—look—that's Will, Mom. WILL?"

"Where?"

"On the ground. Roy, that's Will. Will, that's Roy."

"Hey—how—are you—Will?"

"I'm number ONE!"

"No, don't, Will. Roy, be careful."

"Get him away from me!"

"ROY-Y! ROY-Y! I'LL GIVE YA ROY-Y!"

"Oh, our suitcase came open."

"Get him away! Get the crazy bastard off me!"

"WILL! WILL! GET AWAY FROM HIM! STOP IT PLEASE!"

"YOU GET AWAY FROM HERE, WILL COLE. JACK, CALL THE POLICE!"

"Do—you think—?"

"CALL THEM, JACK!"

"Yes—I guess you're right."

"Hey fella—Hey Will—nice fella, Will—"

"MET 'ER IN TORONTO, DID YA?"

"DRIVER, GIVE ME A HAND!"

"No thanks, sir."

"RUTH! GET THE SUITCASE CLOSED. NEVER MIND ME!"

"Hee-hee, YER CRYIN' NOW, YA LAUGHIN' WHORE!"

"ROY! ROY! COME ON! THE SUITCASE IS IN THE CAR. COME ON!"

"WHAT'RE YA TALKIN' ABOUT, 'COME ON'?? LET GO OF MY LEG! LET GO,—YOU SILLY BASTARD—"

"YOU'RE ALMOST IN, ROY."

"DID IT! GET GOING DRIVER. NO WAIT—HE GOT MY TIE—ST-O-P-P!"

"LET GO OF ROY'S TIE, WILL. HERE ROY, HOLD ONTO ME! PULL, PULL—LOOK OUT ROY!"

"That's all right, his fist hit the door. TAKE OFF DRIVER!"

Oh, me knuckles—me knuckles—dat went all the way up da arm—Which way did dey turn?—Oh, dere dey go! She looks like she's laughin' t'rough da back window. She's laughin' an' cryin'. Well dat's about all I'd expect from dat one. Laughin' an' cryin'. Funny, ain't it?

Anyway, now, look at me, for bruises, an' scrapes. Who came out on top if it wasn't me? I'd like to know. Who? Dat wasn't bad, was it? An' just tink how much more damage I could've done to him, if I lived right next door, here, an' didn't have to run all dat way, across town .

But I didn't get in too many low hits. Dat means they'll prob'ly have children, after all. Well If dey're goin' to turn out lookin' like dat fella, the joke's on dem.

What's this, a squad car? That's Bill 217. He's wearin' his nice new hat, too.

"OK, Will."

"Where were ya?"

"Will, I got a call—"

"A fella an' his girl just attacked me."

"Now—"

"He's from da mainland. You haven't got much time."

"Look, Will—"

"Dat wrist is broke, b'y."

"Will, I'm new, here."

"Never mind dat. Give me a smoke, now, like a good b'y."

"Here! Now, I'm going to be back in five minutes, and you'd better be gone from here."

"How long? Five? Plenty of time. Here. I'll close your door for ya. Dere. So long Bill."

"AND YOU'RE LOVELY, TELL YOUR MOTHER!!"

Now, what're ya all starin' at? You're wonderin' why he didn't haul me off in da car, I s'pose.

Well, see, I don't know if ya remember or not, but dere was a constable who tried dat once, an' dey had to get all new upholstery for da car. Dat new man knows all about dat, an' he's makin' me walk to da station. An' if I don't show up, he'll be out wit' da cuffs. But he knows I'll be dere, 'cause dere's someting about him dat frightens me someting fierce. He's goin' to be a good man.

Now, I hope you've had enough of me, because it's all you're goin' to get—till tomorrow!